# CARRIER OF THE DEAD

# CARRIER OF THE DEAD

## P. N. GRANOZIO

**To order additional copies of this book, contact:**
Xlibris Corporation
1-888-795-4274
www.Xlibris.com
Orders@Xlibris.com
119962

# CONTENTS

"The Forecastle"

## Author's dedication:

This book is a tribute to the men and women who served on board the USS George H.W. Bush CVN-77 air craft carrier. The Deck Department of the 2011 deployment. I would like to thank the following shipmates: Tyler Norland, Rene Barrier, Jose Collado, Danny Roblino, Justine Seybert, Andrew Barich, Ruffle Guieb, Ryan Dorsey, Mr. Nicholson, Tommy Ward, Ralph Gibeson, Randall Cribb, D. Eddington, Brendon Drew, Derrick Luphner, Scott Cloar, Erikka Dallmeyer, Mr. Rodger Walker, my cousin Todd Gibson Jr. and all the sick fucks that encouraged me to finish this story.

Most importantly I would like to dedicate this book to my cousin whose creative imagination has inspired me to complete the book; Billy Gibson.

Character artwork design and concept by: Erikka Dallmeyer.
Graphic Art design and direction created by P. N. Granozio

This story takes place on an air craft carrier. No specific carrier was used in the writing of this novel. It is up to the fans and readers to decide...

# Prologue

The dark clouds approached as the distant lightning flickered its electric show. Only thunder could be heard as it rolled past. The crewmember walked slowly on the flight deck, his arms swung stiff as he dragged his right foot. In his pocket was an iPod playing the R.E.M. song "It's the End of the World as We Know It" on loop. The black earphones played loud in his ears, drowning out the environment all around him. His distinct dark blue coveralls were all cut and torn up. Only the words GRANOZIO stained the white letters in blood, the last remembrance of his human last name from his military coveralls. His lower jaw hung low, preventing his mouth from closing as blood drooled out. The right ribs were showing like rotten cages as his intestines dragged on the ground, leaving the horrific blood trail. Often he would stumble on them, trying to concentrate on what he was doing. A massive cut was exposing his brains as blood rushed out down his face, creating a vision of where he has been. He emitted agonizing growls and snarls as blood oozed out his mouth. With menacing moans, he cried out as his arms stretched and tried to grab his next victim.

It was the lone fire of a single bullet that entered his forehead and out the other side, creating a hole. Through the hole, the silhouette killer stared as another infected fell to his knees. A few seconds and it was over. His reign was finished as he fell to his knees and lay hard on his stomach, his face smacking flat on the flight deck as he let out his final groan.

Only four humans remained. From about six thousand people that inhabited the floating steel city, these were the last survivors. There was the sight of rotten decay of death all around. Even after all that has happened, after all that could have been prevented to control the situation, now things got out of hand. There were so many thoughts and doubts going through Timmy's mind as he reloaded his 9MM pistol. Shaking from his nerves, he dropped a few bullets. "Don't fucking waste any of them, shipmate!" Boats shouted as he picked them off the ground and throwing the bullets to Timmy. A slight smile twisted on his lips as Timmy carefully put the bullets back in the clips.

The final stand would not take place in some old Western town or a dramatic city street. The final stand would take place onboard an aircraft carrier. Near the forward port-left-side on the flight deck, only the last remains of what was left of the fire was keeping the tortured at bay from their prey. Their screams were annoying to anyone within ear range. The howls and shrieks sent a cold feeling into the survivors' souls. "I don't want to become like you. I will not end up like that!" Timmy shouted at the infected as if they gave a shit what he was saying to them. Boats accepted the inevitability that as soon as the fire went out, The Dead will kill what was left of the survivors. Dark cold nothing was looking down upon them, ready to devour any sign of the struggle of the living.

Timmy looked at Boats with desperation as if Boats was going to get them out of this. Maybe some secret exit or extra clips would appear for their last stand on earth. Only four remained. Only four survivors were left, a boatswain's mate, a deck seaman, a master chief, and an injured female pilot officer. No reward, no congratulations, why should there be? After all, what grief should the last people standing come to grips with? What reward is it to see the remaining survivors turn and eat each other?

Desperation turned to anger, anger turned to hate, and soon hate turned into survival. One of the infected was shoved into the fire, creating a bridge so the others can cross the flames. The once-human infected screamed in pain as they stepped on him, pushing his body between the fires and smoldering flight deck. The sound of crackling and popping flesh on the flames reminded Timmy of times when his father would throw frozen meat on the grill. How disgusting this sound was now! The sizzling noise of a skillet was more what Boats thought of. Then they pressed their weight on the thing.

The sound of fire and flesh made that destined mass press on their feet. "Here they come! Make these shots count!" Boats shouted as he cocked the 9MM back, ready to unload. "COME ON, YOU FUCKERS! I AIN'T GOT ALL FUCKING NIGHT!" Boats screamed.

Just in front of the fire, three of them stopped about twenty feet from the undead whose eyes were missing, teeth broken from unsuccessfully biting through metal or worn from chewing on bones. The decaying of their skin was as if they were walking the earth for over hundreds of years. Their hands were not that of a human but more like rotting limbs ready to fall off. They could not see at all. Their eyes were black and white, with fungus growing where human eyeballs once gazed and were now replaced with a horrible curse. Their heads turned in every direction, but their smell was not that good either. However, their hearing was acute. Just the sound of the fire crackling was enough to alert their senses.

The crack of the gun echoed, loud enough to get their attention to where only two now stood, and behind them were hundreds, if not thousands, of the cursed. How could God allow such an abomination to walk the earth? But the survivors remembered once again that it was not God who created them. It was the mere mortals who wanted to play God. There were so many of the dead and so little of the living. Two infected crouched on all fours, smelling the one that was shot, and they and ran on toward the loud noise. Timmy stood there waiting to time his shots—he remembered what Boats told him about wasting shots.

One of them jumped arms extended, leaping fifteen feet in the air like a lion pouncing on its prey, toward Timmy. As the cursed descended on the human, another loud gunshot echoed. The cursed one got pushed back by the force of a 12-gauge shotgun pumping pellets through his skull. Master Chief grinned as he pumped another shell into the chamber. There was nothing left of the undead's face, only a headless mess of splattered blood and brain pieces. *One more to kill, then we will battle our final stand,* Boats thought to himself. *These must have been the scouts before another wave. No rest now. Once this last one lies before their feet, the fury of the devil himself will bestow only misery on the remaining.* Boats aimed carefully as the last one charged like a raging bull, grunting with infected saliva spewing from its mouth. Every move he made excreted piles of blood dripping from his mouth. Boats aimed down his sights and fired, jerking his arm back, and the cursed was shot down as the bullet pierced the skull into the spine. "Reload! Reload, everyone! Here they come!" Boats cried.

Echoes of the dead drowned the mere scream coming from Boats. They ran as fast as they could as if it was their last meal. The undead charged, trampling over each other, often fighting and pushing and biting each other, just to get a taste of the last human flesh. The horde was charging.

Master Chief reloaded the shotgun once again. With a cigar in the left side of his mouth, this salty fucker would not go down easily. His old-school ways were uncanny. Even now as they advanced, he glanced toward the west to watch the sunset and remembered how things got so fucked up. The talent this old man had clearly showed—superb marksmanship. He never flinched a timed shot as he just decapitated three of them with his 12-gauge pump-action shotgun. Still for a second, his eyes did not gaze away from the sun as it crept below the ocean horizon. From the east, a storm was building, the approaching lighning lit up the thunder clouds.. All that remained was the invasion of the darkness and the introduction of death.

Master Chief was expected to retire from the navy after thirty-three years of service. This was not how he imagined things would go. But he accepted his fate that his last days on earth would be with a fight, the bloody fight from the living dead. "Lieutenant! MAAM I need you here with me. Don't go UA on me yet!" Even in the face of death, this crusty master chief still honored military bearing.

She nodded her head and checked her rounds to make sure she had enough for the end. A previous explosion sent a large piece of shrapnel through her leg, her left thigh. It was evident that if it was pulled out, it would cut off a major blood artery, possibly killing her within minutes. Her job now was to load up the guns and pass them to what was left of the survivors. Her leg throbbed in pain, but she guessed that it was better than being a walking lifeless being. Empty clips were thrown next to her, and she did her best to reload them. Her thumbs soar from clippin the bullets in the empty rounds.

Lt. Jennifer McCormick was a helicopter pilot in her fifth year attached to the carrier squadron. She was looking forward to the port visits and often imagined of how proud her parents thought of her. But now things were different. She must regroup and grasp her reality and accept that she was not flying helicopter planes anymore. She was killing the cursed. Brushing her blonde hair away from her face, she thought that nothing must distract her from reloading ammo. Every bullet she dropped was one less minute alive on earth.

Timmy and Boats made every shot count, but even then, it did not matter. They were outnumbered, outmatched, outclassed and soon damn near out of ammo.

Dead bodies lay beneath their feet while hundreds still charged onward. "How many you got left, Timmy?" Boats asked. Timmy held up only five fingers. Boats grinned and only held up four. How could so many rounds be wasted? They were not. The evidence of dead bodies reassured any doubt. It was hard to fathom killing people you worked with—these were the final remains of the carrier crew onboard the American aircraft carrier. With a crew of almost six thousand, dead bodies lay scattered all over the ship. Like cowboys in the old West against outlaws, they were in the middle of gun smoke hazing the air. Constant groaning and screaming of the undead with the repeating bangs of discharged ammo drowned the air with sound.

They were all shipmates, friends, coworkers. They were all once normal before all this happened. The pride of American military might, the aircraft carrier was the gem of the United States. It was considered a fortress and floating city, and nothing alive would dare challenge its military presence. It was the undead that no one saw coming. Thousands of them infecting the entire ship, running, screaming, hungry for human flesh. It was hard to imagine that at one time they were sailors proud of their jobs. Many of them often had families back home, waiting for them, and they probably have no idea what happened to them. Boats saw some names on the uniforms just before he popped their heads off and remembered some of the them, some of their stories before they were mindless, walking infected creatures.

. . . . .

She was probably getting ready to meet her husband when the ship pulled into home port. She prepared her kids and was excited to see him leave that iron vessel. Running toward him, she kissed him and embraced him in her arms. The thoughts of sexual gestures between their eyes admitted the passion and desire both would have looked forward to that night. These were realities to imagine if things were normal. Her name was Kristine. Too bad her husband now lay with his head blown off because he was infected. Now she will only have his memory, his pictures. This was the curse of all of the crewmembers.

He was a single father, gone through a bitter divorce. His oldest daughter, now eighteen, took care of the family while he made her proud of serving his country. She wrote to him often through e-mail and told him of her college grades. Now he had become infected, and his curse infected many others. His body lay at the feet of Timmy and Boats.

He was a new father, leaving her so young with the hope and promise of returning home to protect the one thing he loves most, his family. He held picture of them in his front pocket from when they went to Hawaii, she laughing as she kisses him on the boat they rented. They watched a perfect sunset with the calm waves, and they had precious lust for each other. The picture she took while she carefully held the camera and kissed him now has blood splats all over it. His wedding ring was still on his finger with her picture tattooed on his upper left chest. Her beauty, her smile, her eyes forever etched on his skin. His name was Michael. He lay missing the other arm which was brutally severed from the bullets that hit him during the wave of the attack just a few hours ago. His body lay with the rest.

This was the agony of the cursed. Many stories untold, many lives affected, many innocent sailors, both females and males, enlisted and officer, so many people forgotten many days during the attacks. Only memories faint from uniforms their last names sewed on them, and the occasional wedding ring haunted the walking infected.

. . . . .

Timmy yelled at boats, "Boats, snap out of it! Remember when I asked you to kill me if I ever turned?" Boats acted like he didn't hear as he neared only two shots left. Timmy yelled again, "Boats, I know you fucking hear me! You remember what you promised me if I ever turned?" Boats nodded and already knew what Timmy was going to ask him to do. His last shot he pointed toward the cursed and hesitated. Boats knew that if he did not do this, he was going to end up killing his buddy after he turned. They had already been through so much death and destruction. It was only at the end that Timmy and Boats put aside their differences to have one thing in common, survive and be the last.

Boat's face accepted what fate lay before them both. The infected ran forward on to their last meal, their mouths salivating blood as they got anxious. Boats turned his last shot toward Timmy. He thought how strange it was to look down the sights and not see an infected. Boats screamed, "Timmy, we do this together!"

Without hesitating, Timmy drew his last shot and aimed it at Boats.

"We had a great ride!" Boats yelled. Looking directly at Timmy, he could hear hundreds coming within feet of tearing both of them to shreds. LT. McCormick was unaware of what was happening and Master Chief could see what was about to unfold. There was no way he could stop this suicide. His screams could not be heard, nor could he prevent how Timmy and Boats were going to end their lives. An unfamiliar humming drew close. Was this another evolution of them? The sound got louder and louder, almost shaking the ground. Fear was going to take over. It had to have been mere seconds apart. The last round was ready to enter the chamber ordered to serve its final purpose.

Before that was allowed, actions had to be executed. Rather than turn to the direction of the loud noise, Timmy smiled and said, "It's too bad. Tonight was pizza night." Both slightly laughed, and with his last sigh of breath, he counted out loud. The metallic click of the final cock assured them both that all this would be over in a matter of seconds.

Boats closed his weak eye concentrating his final shot at the forehead of Timmy.

Boats mimicked his lips saying *three*, and they aimed at each other. *Two*, the final round was clicked into the chamber and the safety was clicked off. *One*, the firing of guns cracked the loud echo as the bullet was ignited, it fired. Pushing through the barrel the gun cracked as the sonic boom bullet was headed for Timmy's skull.

In an instant Timmy's aim was flawless. Directed at Boat's head as well, the final execution was serving one determined purpose. To kill each other before the horde got to them.

# BEFORE THE INFECTION

# Chapter 1

## *ASSIGNMENTS*

Four bells rang loud, and with that, the call to wake-up was announced. John Timmy, a young eighteen-year-old kid from a country-boy lifestyle, rubbed his eyes. "Get the fuck up, shipmates. We got two days before we leave on deployment. We have much to do," Boats said with disgruntled tones in his voice. His real name was hard to pronounce, so every one called him Boats for short because of his job. He was a boatswain's mate second class in the navy. Often, that word *shipmate* was used to just offend people, and Boats was good at offending them, especially the new guys fresh from boot camp. He was twenty two years old, but his military haircut made his age look younger.

It was not easy growing up with three first names. Jonathon Michael Timothy, now in the navy, would have to deal with it on a regular basis. It was an eager wait of only two more days until deployment would begin. Stuff he only read about in school he was going to see. Up till morning quarters, his phone must have gotten a signal. It was difficult to get cell phone signals, a carrier being entirely metal. It was a text from his girlfriend, Jane. His sweetheart. He thought much of how the both of them conquered the popular social challenge of high school. But all that changed in the real world. Her picture appeared with a text saying, "Can't see you tonight. I have to work. So sorry miss you." This was the third time she blew him off. Already Timmy was looking at his watch, and the seconds felt like hours. The day has just started. Why can't it end now?

. . . . .

"Damn, e-mail is slow as shit!" Master Chief screamed as his computer froze. Hitting it was not going to make things better. He often remembered a time when the navy was nothing but a paper trail, before there were computers destroying his career. A man of his age had to adapt with how the navy had changed. Everything was going digital. So must he if he was to have a job. On the wall he often stared at the picture of the extension of his house. Once retired, this was his project, he thought to himself.

No more of this political crap he dealt with. Throughout his office, there were outstanding decorations and metals he received while on tour at different places. Some were proud memories. Others were laced with the guilt of how cutthroat and lowball his job made him become. Backstabbing many of those who helped him get to his rank, Master

Chief did what was necessary to thrive in his naval career. His easy office desk job was the navy's way of thanking this old dog for his wisdom, but newer, younger personal were putting him out of a job.

These snot-nosed kids straight out of the officer academy, trying to tell a master chief how to do his job. This caused conflict with his promotions. In his last duty station on the *USS Boone*, some ensign not even twenty-two years old attempted to tell Master Chief how to correctly discipline junior sailors. The altercation escalated when the young buck tried to pull rank on him. The officer ended up with a ring indentation on his forehead, of the master chief logo. Master Chief hit him so hard, it took a week for the mark to go away. This officer often got smirks and laughs but never walked in the same passageways as the master chief.

NCIS was involved in the investigation of enlisted and officer assault. Favored by the skipper of Master Chief's leadership, the captain was highly pissed off at the ensign for reporting the incident. The young officer was recommended for TAD orders to Afghanistan, signed, and shipped out immediately by the commanding officer.

As far as the old dog goes, his career was over, forced out to finish the rest of his time doing office paperwork on shore duty.

The phone rang. It was Master Chief's boss. "Yes, sir," he said with a fake smile.

His department head, Commander, answered with regret, "Master Chief, there is an aircraft carrier in need of a person of your rank and leadership. However, I denied your application due to your high temper and the last stunt you pulled at your last command. You know that officer you assaulted? I was very good friends with his father who retired with a star."

Silence grew for a few seconds, and Master Chief replied, "Then why are you calling me, sir?"

Commander's voice changed with anger, saying," It seems your career has far surpassed people whom you have affected over the years. The commanding officer of that ship has requested you to finish your service on board the carrier set to deploy in two days. Pack up your shit, pick up your orders, and get the hell out of my sight!"

Without out even a goodbye, he hung up, and Master Chief stood up and felt alive. His passion was the sea. Now he had one more chance to fix all the wrongs, help the crewmembers and act more like a mentor, teach the next generation his lessons of life.

He was stocky built African American man. His bald head was his way of hiding his white hair and receding hairline. Packing up his office, he noticed that the last thing that remained was a picture of his ex whom he loved so very much. But he loved his navy even more. Enough to become astray from his family and forcing his wife to leave him and take from him everything he had. But that was so long ago. He grinned with his cigar and threw the picture in the box, saying "I will make things right. Now where the fuck is my cigar cutter?"

. . . . .

"Mother, will you stop already?" Lieutenant Jenny McCormick laughed as she finished her last-minute packing. Her beautiful figure was what most women desired. She could eat anything she wanted and never gain weight. Often she would take advantage of her bikini-like body and flirt her way. Her decision to become a helicopter pilot was to disobey her mother and father who hoped she would become a doctor or a lawyer. Never did they think their little princess would fly for the military. A competitive woman, she insisted on finishing up her time in the navy and travel the world.

Once her mother, her best friend, almost lost her because of her ex and the entire tangled web he created. His trust and broken promises only made Jenny realize how cruel the world really was. It was almost two years since the incident that almost cost Jenny her life.

. . . . .

*Her mother often remembers the fateful night that forever changed her life.*

His drinking was uncontrollable, his voice filled with disgusting gestures of violence and false demons he was hiding. And Jenny's denial was typical, always blaming herself why he hated her so much. The last time she saw him was that night he tried to kill her.

An innocent text from another woman was found on his phone as he showered. That fucker got caught, and Jenny knew the time and place. Showing up to the hotel, Jenny caught him with the other woman he was fucking.

This other woman screamed with pleasure, with his hand around her neck, getting penetrated in a rough manner. This was how she liked it as she dug her nails into his back. He had her pined up against the wall as she wrapped her legs around him, screaming with pleasure.

He saw Jenny, and she ran out the door. That's when he ran after her. The fight was near the car. His breath reeked of alcohol. He did not want to lose her, and all hope of ever being with her was lost. *No,* he thought to himself, *if I cannot have you, then no one will.* With a quick thrust around her neck, he forced his way in between her legs. The betrayal of this beast was too much to bear. The more she resisted, the harder he punched her. Grabbing her by her neck, he held her down as he raped her.

Almost leaving her for dead, the police arrived with guns drawn. How did they know? The evidence that an attack happened moments ago lay all over the backseat as she lay motionless. Her phone was on the passenger floor. She must have dropped it during the assault and activated speed dial to her mother. She heard everything, the attack, the grunting, the struggle. It was her mother who called the police, and they traced her phone. This monster would not hurt anyone again. Her face was beaten to a bloody pulp after what that animal did to her. But that was all memories meant to be lost forever.

. . . . .

They were no longer together, and this made her mother happy. This was what she wanted. Her daughter was back. They were together again as it was before her life was turned upside down. It was all her mother had, with her father always at work, with no desire for her at all. The suspect of an affair had been brought to the privacy of the bedroom. Both agreed to stay together to support their daughter. After all she went through, both mother and father vowed never to hurt Jenny again. So the fake curtain lay before Jenny's eyes.

Her mother knew that once she left for deployment, Jenny's father would move out. Her feelings toward him were that of a stranger you see across the street. She could not remember the last time he ever showed affection toward her. The divorce was processed. Poor Jenny had no idea how lies were invented to keep her morale positive.

Jenny kissed her father who was reading his *Wall Street*. All that talk about stocks upset him, but he always reminded her how proud he was of her. But he was not proud at all. All that college money wasted. The new car she wrecked two years ago, and he was still fixing the lawsuit she created. The hospital bills her ex caused. Now she flies helicopters. He was not impressed with her career choice. But if he did not support her, she would run even farther from him. This was how she coped with life. Spoiled by her father, she would always get her way. "Jenny, let's get the car packed and get you to the airport. We don't want you to miss your flight," Father said.

Jenny smiled with her naïve personality. Checking her room one last time to make sure she did not forget anything, she remembered growing up in this room, the doll house, Barbie dolls, and tea parties both her parents enjoyed with her. But she was all grown up now, and it was time to go to work. Shutting off the light, she shut the door. And with that, the door of her childhood was shut as well as she remembered how easy life was being innocent. Forgetting how to act like a child, she headed out the door. Her father was waiting in the car, and she thought to herself that it was time to grow up.

. . . . .

"Why did you not inspect them, Boats?" This was the question the chief had when he caught one of the deck seamen unshaven for morning quarters. Boats shrugged his shoulders because if he told chief the truth that they all went drinking all night and got in late and showing up with a hangover, everyone would be in trouble.

Boats replied, "It's my fault. I'll discipline them." He only said what the chief wanted to hear, hoping that would be enough.

The chief turned to Boats, saying, "I want to see their paperwork that you disciplined them on my desk before you go to lunch!"

*Fuck, there was no getting around this,* Boats thought. Frustrated, he screamed to the chief, "I got this! I'll handle it! Go back to the chiefs' mess and get some coffee. If I need you, I know where to find you." That was enough to get him out of there. Every day was like this with this chief. Does this guy had a life? All he did was live onboard. Everyone had a life, but this asshole was all Joe Navy.

Boats served five years in the navy already and was now on his second deployment attached to the ship's company. It was hard being a leader now, no more acting like a child. If there was more help in the department, there would not be so much pressure on Boats. "Cindy, come with me. We have some areas we need to clean."

24

Cindy was a young woman not even twenty years old, and many guys desired to have a one-night stand with her, but her lust was set on someone she worked with. Her flirtatious gestures were for the attention of Timmy. Boats saw the signs. He did his best to keep the two of them apart. Boats knew little of Timmy and saw Cindy as causing trouble. Boats gave Cindy a friendly thought as they walked through the narrow passageways, "Cindy you should find yourself a nice civilian guy."

Her laugh was even flirtatious as she responded, "I know, but I love the attention. Do you know if Timmy has a girlfriend?"

Boats grinned. Even if he did, he feared that she would still try something with him. He just shook his head. "We have a new check-in. Her name is Justine. She will be here around eleven, so get her some sheets and make sure she has a locker and blankets," he said as they went to clean out the fan room.

. . . . .

"Master Chief, welcome aboard." A friendly hand extended from Cindy Walkers who was standing quarter deck watch. Master Chief looked her up and down, trying to find fault in her uniform. He remembered this was a time for change. He politely gestured toward the entrance of the ship and grabbed his bags, reporting to his new duty station. On board an aircraft carrier, shipmates busied preparing the ship for the deployment.

Twelve noon was upon the ship, and the car pulled up to the gate where families dropped off their loved ones. Because of the security force, it was evident that civilian vehicles were kept a great distance from the nuclear carrier. The black Buick drove past the great ship, and out the window, Jenny saw where her new home would be the next half year. Talk was uncomfortable with both parents in the car. Her father drove as her mother stared out the window, having no desire to look at him. Pulling at the security checkpoint, Jenny presented her military ID, and they proceeded forward to the airfield where her new vehicle awaited, the military helicopter squadron attached to the carrier. Her two girlfriend officers waited at the entrance to the airfield building. Jenny must have texted them that she was minutes away.

Her mother with thought of the night that animal almost killed Jenny. Words could not describe how hard it was to do nothing, how tough it was to be completely helpless. What made her think of that moment now? *How stupid can you be?* she thought to herself. Blocking any memory of that night, she turned to Jenny who was sitting in the backseat, smiling out the window at her two friends. And she had the pleasant memory of when Jenny was six years old, her first bus ride to school, and the same smile was etched in that moment of time forever. Fighting back the tears, her mother controlled her voice to disguise she was weak. A strong woman she must always be. "Jenny, looks like your friends are waiting for you."

Jenney's father was already outside opening the trunk of the Buick and getting out the bags. One of the bags was not completely closed. The zipper must have been stuck. He grabbed the end, tugging it in both directions until it opened more. Something caught his eye in the bag, something he had not seen in ten years, a picture of Jenny at her birthday with her mom and dad happy and laughing. *How could things get so bad? Admit to your conscience. You fucked things up. You tore your wife away from you. Fucking eyes tend to get watery when you admit you were the cause.* "Nothing I can do now," he said out loud. Fixing the bag and grabbing the rest of Jenny's stuff, he closed the trunk to see Jenny and her mother embracing each other. How he wished he could embrace them both, but things would get complicated. *Better I wait,* his conscience told him. The minutes felt like days, and soon Jenny grabbed the courage to approach her father. Her mother ran back in the car, not saying another word. "You call me when you can, and e-mail me every day. I love you, sweetheart," her father with a stern voice told her. Her hug was something he did not get very often. But nothing would tear them apart.

The sudden whip of a wing rotating faster and faster soon grew into deafening repetitious thumps. It was time to go as her co-pilots called on Jenny to hurry up. Last-minute checks had to be completed before Lt. Jennifer McCormick could fly out and meet the carrier tomorrow. The air crew was testing the engines for the helicopter squadrons. Jenny grabbed her bags and watched as they both left the gate entrance. It was too hard for her to hold back tears. Jenny sobbed because she loved them so much. *It's time to grow up. Time to do my job.* She approached the check-in desk, and a young woman smiled, "Good afternoon, ma'am. What squadron are you with?"

With a grin, she said "Yes, my name is Lieutenant Jenny McCormick, and that's my helicopter." She pointed out the window. The young woman looked jealous and thought how a pretty girl like her could get a job like that. *Slut.* Grabbing her paperwork, Jenny headed to her living quarters for the night. Tomorrow will be a long day.

Nothing was spoken when Jenny's parents drove home. The awkward silence had to stop. Mother reached over to select a channel on the XM radio. It was a familiar song, and Mother hummed out loud, maybe to annoy him. Well, it worked. He changed the station to the news, hoping to hear about the carrier leaving tomorrow. Jenny often bragged how a camera crew was going to document the deployment. With her flirtatious ways, she loved the camera, her father thought. A slight grin was halted when the newsman spoke, "This is David. Behind me is the location where they found motionless bodies everywhere. A massive investigation is underway to explain what exactly happened. The local government is working effortlessly to confirm if this is in fact a new virus, the likes of which no one has ever seen. Dead corpses have been discovered, and there has been no explanation of what went wrong. We have been informed that for our own protection, we are not allowed to enter the site. Some witnesses stated that some of them were actually feeding on—"Mother was annoyed and turned off the radio. She did not want to make the ride home pleasurable either. Still the silence was common the rest of the way home.

· · · · ·

"Don't be late tomorrow. You don't want to be that guy who missed the ship, and if you drink, call me. I want to show you squids how to handle a drink," Boats said.

A slight chuckle was heard through the ranks. "Attention to muster!" Everyone perked up, and with the salute, Boats yelled the most favorite word, "POST!" After a quick return salute, Timmy ran off. "Not much time," he said as he hurried off the ship. As Timmy ran down the enlisted bow, his phone vibrated. Pulling it out of his pocket, he found that it was another disappointing text from his girlfriend. "I wanted to see you b4 you go. I have to work late and school. Email me. Love you."

His feelings hurt as he reached in his front pocket and pulled out a small box. He opened it. The shiny two-karat diamond sparkled as the sun reflected on it. Tonight was supposed to be his proposal. The reservations were already set at a restaurant he could barely afford on E-3 pay. "Timmy!" a soft voice cried out his name. It was his co-worker Cindy Walkers. He closed the engagement ring box and slid it in his pocket as she ran to catch up to him. Her looks was very pleasing to the eye, short mini skirt with a tight pink top and her long brown hair brushed down to her shoulders. She resembled Selena Gomez.

This cutie used her flirtatious ways and looked sexy. "Hey, Timmy, what are you doing on the last day before we leave?" Cindy Walker asked.

Timmy smiled and said, "Nothing now, I mean, I had plans, but well, hey are you hungry?" He smiled. "I know a great place we could get some great food. In fact, I got reservations." And they walked to his car.

# Chapter 2

## *THE TRIP TO NO WHERE*

David looked at his watch with frustration, and his patience grew short. After a long flight in from New York to some remote country, the jet lag was finally kicking in. "Yeah, big story my ass," he mumbled to himself. The scruffy hair on his face and bags under his eyes were appearing to become noticeable. Maybe a hot bath was all he needed. Hell no. What David needed was a drink. Something to calm his nerves.

Working on a story from an anonymous person about local people getting sick and disappearing was hardly worth the three-thousand-mile trip. But who was he to argue while everyone got to travel to celebrity parties and exotic trips to tropical locations? He was in his early thirties and was working for a new publishing company from New York. Newspapers were no match for the modern Internet craze. Radio was replaced by satellite radio, and his employers owned a radio station. There was so much competition on stories that now anyone with a cell phone could become a reporter. The overnight fame was just another competitor David Schwimmer had to deal with. He and his crew of two were on a hot story of local disappearances. Billy Gibson and Caleigh, the two interns that were just trying to get some on-the-job training, assisted David on his travels.

"You know walking across the street with a map is a sure sign we are out-of-towners!" Billy screamed.

Caleigh looked up just to make sure no car was going to hit her. Quickly running towards Billy, she smiled, saying, "The local bar is the best place to find out a lead about this story. Many of the locals travel through the woods at night, but some have not been coming back."

David sighed, all but knowing that this story was a dead end. "So great. We will meet tonight 9:00 pm at that bar. I'm going back to the hotel and relax in this god-awful heat. Fucking no AC! What a shitty hellhole!" David vented at his watch.

Billy checked his gear, making sure nothing was missing. Overhearing David and Caleigh's conversation, he quickly changed the subject, "I will call the company and inform them of this place. Now if I can only get a signal."

Billy was a young kid. He considered himself an adventurer. His quiet personality was only to those he didn't know. His hair was growing kind of shaggy, but his smile was his charmer. College parties and frat houses were how he survived. After getting his associate's degree in telecommunications, it was now the real world, to get a job and travel.

Caleigh, a twenty-year-old cutie, wanted to travel and help others. Her thick curly red hair and green eyes made heads turn when she walked into a room. Rather than bask in the attention, she kept her hair in a ponytail under a baseball cap. A tomboy, she was called, and she could outdrink most men on the table.

It was nearly 9:00 pm, and the bar was full of local workers, laughing and talking about the workday. Outdated music from the jukebox played while a drunken couple danced alone. David entered the bar and took off his hat. Waving from a distance were Caleigh and Billy. It was clear enough that the both of them already had too much to drink. "Jesus Christ, guys, what time did you both start drinking?" David asked as he slid into the booth.

The interruption of hiccups and giggles was enough to make David laugh as Billy was showing Caleigh his tattoos he got when he was in college. "And this one I got on a bet, kind of sucks. Maybe I should get this removed." He unbuttoned his shirt, and there was a tattoo of a skeleton drinking a bottle of tequila with the initials *B. G.* written below in old English. It took up the left side of his chest.

It was apparent by the ten empty shots lined up that they were pretty drunk.

Billy, slurring his words, said, "So I arranged for you to meet this local guy who claims some weird stuff is going on the next village over. Took me a minute, but after I bought him a beer, he agreed to meet you."

"I better not be sent on some bullshit story," David replied. "What time is he going to be here?"

"I think he is here." Billy pointed at the lone man across the bar.

"Where?"

"Sitting there in that booth. He said he was wearing a black ball cap hat, and that's the only guy in the bar wearing one."

"Well, let's get this over with so I can get back home." Chugging his frost beer, David stood up and brought the brew with him. He walked over to the stranger and sat down. The sound of small talk and conversations nearly drowned out the bar.

"Sir?" David began. "Are you the man with—"

"My name is Cooper, and I wanted to let you both know that if I tell you what is going on, your lives may be at danger." Mr. Cooper was an older gentleman. His white hair and wrinkles showed that he worked his entire life. He was skinny with old marine tattoos probably from the Vietnam era.

"What? I don't understand. Please explain."

"People are disappearing, vanishing, and no one knows why. We thought it was local animals, but there is no evidence, so one day as I was fishing, a military boat pulled up to this local village. They did not see me, but I saw them. Armed to the teeth, they forced families, women, and men at gunpoint into their boats. I decided to follow them. Their boats were far faster than my put-put. I eventually lost them downriver but came across a highly fortified base. That's when I turned around and contacted you guys."

"What base? There was no base on any of the maps."

"About seventy-five miles. It won't be on any maps. It's completely restricted, but maybe you guys can get in there."

"Can you take us there?"

"Yes, but . . . we have to leave now."

"Meet me outside in one hour near the only hotel in the town. Me and my crew will be ready. Oh, and we will pay you." Shaking his hand, David folded some American money in his hand and gave it to him.

With the nod from this old man, the two parted ways. Excited, David returned to the table and quickly explained to the other two what was going to happen. Leaving in a hurry, the three of them packed their gear and waited outside.

An old beat-up red 1975 Chevy pickup truck pulled up. The squeak of the brakes was evidence that it's been years since they were checked. "Hop in the back," Cooper said to them. "David, get in the front."

The third gear was rough. It must have been years since this vehicle ever got a transmission fix. Paved roads soon became dirt roads. Dirt roads soon became barely visible brush. Huge branches and overgrown leaves damn near engulfed the trails.

The drive was over an hour. Nothing but woods and thick jungle. Caleigh and Billy were knocked out, spooning and trying to keep warm in the back.

"Were here," Cooper announced. "This is as far as I can take you guys." The truck stopped with the loud rusty brakes, waking up Caleigh and Billy. "Here is a picture of my granddaughter," Cooper went on to say. "She is missing and we all wonder what happened to her. Her name is Lucy . . . If you . . ." His voice cracked as he tried to hold back the tears. "If you see her, please . . ."

"I know," David replied. "It's okay, sir. I already know." He then thought that it would be better if David changed the subject than see this old man cry. His question was to answers he already knew. "Okay now, you said we walk about two miles, and we will find it?"

"Yes, hurry. I will wait here."

"Thank you, sir. Caleigh, Billy, you guys up?"

As they got out of the truck, the old man assured them it was only a two-mile hike then hesitantly drove off. *So much for waiting for us,* David thought. His hand clutched the picture of a little six-year-old girl playing near a local well. *I know that when the picture was taken, this was once a happy family,* David thought.

Billy grabbed the pic and studied it with his glazy eyes. "Looks like my niece."

"Great, now were in the middle of nowhere, and we gotta hike the rest of the way," Caleigh piped in.

"Let's get moving," David said. "Daylight is going to blow our cover."

It was terrible. Thick brush, jungle bugs, and constant humidity were not making this hike any easier. Besides carrying all the gear, two of the crewmembers were still drunk. The sweat spots from the chest, armpits and back made it clear that no one was prepared for the hike. Billy regretted growing his hair like a beach bum. Now it was just annoying.

It had to have been about ninety minutes. Billy threw up two times, and Caleigh kept her hair up in a ponytail because of the chunks she threw up as well.

"Boy, a chainsaw would be useful right about now," Billy said.

"Shut up and keep hacking," David replied. "Caleigh, you okay back there?"

The huffing and short breath from her was a clear sign that she needed to stop carrying all the gear. Then the sign of a machete hitting steel quickly got everyone's attention. The spark alone lit up the night surroundings. It was a metal cross-guard fence they struck. They looked in between the iron-hexed fence, but all was quiet. David quickly put his small flashlight in his mouth and aimed it at a map. "Funny, this is not on the map. According to this, we are here, and this map says its undiscovered land. There is something in there they don't want us to find."

Caleigh and Billy smiled and looked at David on what to do next. It was apparent that David had been in somewhat of the same situation before. Using bolt cutters, he cut a four-section diameter and peeled back the fence. He said, "Both of you don't have to go with me. I am not asking you. However, if we enter this area, which is clearly off-limits, and get caught, I cannot guarantee that things will go smooth."

Caleigh and Billy both smiled as if this adventure would be more fun if danger was involved. The nod was enough.

Inside the perimeter were three iron sheds about twenty feet in length. Each was separated about a hundred feet apart. The height was that of an average two-story building. It was apparent that whatever was being protected was inside these sheds. Bolt cutters to the rescue once again as the back door was broken. No lights, only the ray of the flashlights, were showing the way. They walked down a narrow hall into two swinging doors, and rows of beds were on either side. Bunk beds, a lot of them. As the light shined on them, people awoke. Dazed and confused, they adjusted their eyes to the bright light of the flashlights. All were wearing dirty white hospital gowns. Upon closer look, they looked ill. The pale expressions and skin-and-bones appearance were clear indication that these were not healthy people. Their arms extended, crying for help. David quickly shut the door, got his camera, and started taking pictures.

"Okay, we will get as many pictures as we can, then we will get the hell out of dodge and see if we can ID them to see if they are the missing people," David said. "And we need to check the other two sheds. I suggest we split up. Caleigh and Billy, you both take a shed. We will meet back at the fence in ten minutes. *Ten minutes, understand?*"

After a quick check of their gear, they split up. Caleigh, cutting her lock, threw Billy the bolt cutters and off he was to the last shed. It was the same as the first shed, sick people begging for help. Caleigh's heart fell for them, scrambled through her bag and gave away all her water.

Billy broke the last shed's lock and entered. It was obvious he was a war game fanatic by the way he was standing. His *Halo* game skills were in play now. He was waiting for an ambush or some kind of attack. What he got instead was the groaning of more sick people. This room had many children in it. Crying for their mothers and fathers, no one was there to help them. His light scanned until something caught his eye. "Lucy!" he said. She was dirty and very lean. There was something disturbing seeing a six-year-old child like this. Her upper lip had the dry marks of dry blood from a previous bloody nose. Her thumb in her mouth was a sign that she was craving something to drink. *Nothing to drink,* Billy thought to himself.

After taking the pictures, he was leaving the shed when he heard Lucy cry. Maybe he was reminded of his little niece and how she would curl up next to him and sleep. Her cute ways made him promise to himself that everywhere he went, he would get her a small gift. His thoughts were soon brought back to reality. "Lucy, you're coming with me," Billy said with compassion. He picked her up and wrapped her in his arm. Her squirmy body was aching to get warm. Running out the door, he was struck by her odor, an indication that a clean bath was what she was lacking. Looking at his watch, he realized it was time to leave. As he left the shed, he ran as fast as he could with Lucy. Little tears ran down her face as she cried for her mother. But her instincts were telling her that Billy was helping her. Halfway to the gate, he thought to himself that carrying the gear and the little girl was slowing him down. "Fuck the gear," he said out loud. Dropping it, he focused on getting Lucy to safety.

Her cough was not good. She was gagging, trying to breathe. As he was running, he started patting her on the back to ease her lungs. Looking behind, he was making sure was not followed. Then something caught his eye, a blood trail following him. *I know I wasn't hit.* He checked everywhere until he found the source. Lucy was spitting up blood. He held her back, and before he could react, she threw up blood and mucus all over Billy. All over his face, in his mouth, and all he could taste was whatever this sick girl had in her stomach. "Fuck!" he screamed. He put her on the ground as this crap was all over him, in his eyes, down his shirt. The smell was more than he could bear. It was now him throwing up.

Composing himself, he was determined to get her out of here. He ran and grabbed her and headed for the fence. He had only twenty feet to go when the alarms went off. "OH SHIT! OH MY GOD! WE'RE IN TROUBLE! DAMMIT!" Billy screamed to Lucy. Soldiers soon had David and Caleigh on their knees with their hands above their heads. Weapons drawn, they were ready to shoot the journalists. Spotlights and guard dogs were all active around the compound. Billy thought of his options and decided to hide Lucy and surrender. Putting her in behind the back of a jeep, he kissed her and told her to sleep. Admitting defeat, he raised his hands up in the air for the universal signal of surrender.

. . . . .The Interrogation . . . . .

The three were tied to a chair, and these black figures were not the kind of guys you would want to fuck with. They paced back and forth and did what they do best. "I will ask you again. What were you all doing in the compound?" One of them asked.

"Nothing we were just curious," David replied. "We're tourists. We got lost and found it."

"Bullshit! You were looking for something. You are not leaving until you tell us the truth."

One by one, hours went by, and each was threatened and demanded to tell the truth on who they were and why they were in the area that was clearly off-limits.

Another man entered, addressing himself as Mr. Rene Barrier. The dimmed light hid his identity as he spoke. "I had to fly all the way from my vacation to deal with you guys. You will not leave here until you tell us what the fuck you were doing in a restricted area!"

"We didn't know it was restricted, sir," Billy said.

"BULLSHIT, SON!" Barrier exploded. "And where they hell did you get all that blood on your shirt?"

"I was in a bar fight earlier. You should see what the other guy looks like."

This was getting nowhere. After all their cameras were destroyed and passports returned, they were told that these people were sick, and a few government experiments were required to make them better. It was speculated that a joint government sector was to cure them. David, Caleigh, and Billy were then drugged and woke up on the corner of the local American embassy. No one really knew how long they were there or how many days were missed.

They were made aware that should they pursue any investigation, then the United States would be informed that these three Americans broke into a government facility. All three were believed to have had no contact with the sick. There was nothing more that could be said.

"So now what do we do?" Caleigh said, sitting in the main office.

The secretary called David over to the phone. David knew what was going to happen. The corporate bosses were on the phone. "Hello," he said.

"Boy, you three have caused us a world of shit. You know that?" his boss said.

"Yes, sir, I understand."

"Do you know how much time and money we had to dish out because the three of—you know, I'm not even blaming them. I'm blaming you for your Indiana Jones stunt!"

"Sir, I am sorry, and I guess when I return I will clean out my office."

"I should leave you there, and you can find your own way back. The issue is that you have been with us from the beginning, and just because your reputation exceeds your ego, don't even think that I can't fire your ass right now!

"I don't know what the hell went on there. Maybe you're telling the truth. Maybe you were led to a dead end. It's over now, so forget this dead-end story. You will not be coming home."

David was silent and didn't say a word until his boss was finished.

His boss continued, "You will report to an aircraft carrier located in the east Indian Ocean. The aircraft carrier pulled out a week ago for a maiden deployment. All you got to do is spend a month with the crew and interview them on everyday life. A major network will buy the rights to our footage and make it into a documentary. Do not fuck this up, David! We already got a nice check from them. This will include your flight tickets to get you guys out there. Get this done right and let's put this crap behind us."

"I understand, sir," David replied. "Thank you and I will not fuck up. I will make things right." He hung up the phone, and a sigh of relief was exhaled. It was like having a second chance. Walking over to meet Caleigh and Billy, he grinned.

"So how did the conversation go?" Caleigh asked. "Are we going to jail?"

"Kind of, depends if you think that's where we are going," David replied.

"I don't get it," Billy said, confused.

"We will be getting a paycheck within two days so we can buy equipment and supplies from corporation," David began. "So you all ready for the good news?"

Billy and Caleigh smiled and rolled their eyes.

"We're going on an aircraft carrier that left about a week ago," David went on. "They are going to fly us out there on the first available flight, and we will be there for about a month. All we got to do is document life onboard, mingle with the crew, and once we get all the footage, a major network channel will buy our footage and give us credit for the documentary."

"This could be fun!" Caleigh said. "Beats being out in the jungle."

"Look we have a job to do," David said. "We . . . err, I have been told not to fuck this up."

"Okay, but what about these people?" Billy asked.

David put his head down and shook his head. "Let it go. We were told by corporate not to pursue."

Billy, already annoyed how the last three days transpired, took his cap off and threw it across the room. "This is bullshit! What, so we forget what we saw? How can you be human and still forget all them people?"

"Look, I know your frustrations, but this is over my head," David replied. "We're lucky to even make it out alive. We all could have been prisoners or, worse, dead. Forget about it, and let's fix our relationship with corporate. Everyone understand?"

Billy thought of Lucy and how sick she was. His escape with her ran through his mind over and over again. Was that the smartest thing, putting her in the truck? A dark chill overcame his mind. There was nothing he could do now. "I hope you know that you will all have to live with this," Billy said.

Caleigh looked startled at Billy as he stood up. "Oh my god, Billy. You're bleeding?" She went to grab a napkin.

Billy looked on the ground and saw the blood spatters on his shoe. He wiped it and held his head back. "It's nothing. Just a nosebleed," Billy said.

David wore a look of concern and said, "Hey, you going to be okay for the flight out on COD to the aircraft carrier?"

Caleigh pushed harder on the napkin as the blood slowed down from Billy's nose. "Dude, I will be fine," he said. "It's probably the climate change. Let's get a hotel and wait till the check comes. I need a drink anyways."

Walking out the door, Billy could feel liquid buildup in his throat. Hacking up a congested spit, he aimed for the street corner and spat. Blood was the only thing that came up and hit the concrete curb. There was no mucus buildup, just a huge blood spat. "What the hell?" For a second he thought, he saw it move. "I must be tired. Now I'm seeing things." Shaking his head, he caught up with David and Caleigh. He put his arms around Caleigh and David, saying "So we get to the carrier. Will we be able to get drunk when we hit port with them?"

# Chapter 3

## *THE FIRST INCIDENT*

A few days have passed since David and his crew arrived onboard the aircraft carrier. Things took a lot of getting used to. Small quarters, constant schedule, and the annoyance of always being escorted by a navy personnel to assure that no security would be breached. Billy was not getting any better with his coughing-up-blood incident. It was only getting worse. Sharp pains in his stomach made it unbearable to even keep food in his stomach. Wiping his face with the cold water, he noticed even more blood dripping down the silver sink into the drain.

Billy managed to keep this quiet, but how much more could he handle? "I got to see the doctor. But fuck it! Job comes first," Billy said to his reflection then looked at his watch. "Crap, I'm going to be late." He ran out the bathroom to get his clothes.

Today was the interview with some of the ship's company department crewmembers. The public affairs officer, who dealt with all media and news about the ship, had scheduled an appointment on the forecastle. It was the gem of the ship. Located just 2 decks below the bow of the flightdeck, this is where the massive anchors were housed. The constant cleaning and preservation was evident that the men and women who worked onboard showed a lot of pride in their job.

Boats just got the word that a news crew would be interviewing some sailors for the time being. After numerous ass chewing by his chief, he was not going to make the same mistake of getting caught with his pants down with a dirty space.

"Can you believe this guy?" Timmy said. "Going to make us come back to lunch an hour early just to clean a space we already did two hours ago."

The small conversations were cut short when Boats entered the area. Cindy Walkers was already getting the hang of how things worked on the ship. She basically did nothing until Boats or someone higher in rank showed up, then she acted as if she was working the whole time.

There was little Boats could do from keeping Cindy away from Timmy. During working hours, it was easy. But when the work was over, these two were always together. Perhaps they were trying to be professional at work, but everyone knew they were dating.

Timmy and Cindy both noticed a middle-aged man, a young redhead female, and a shaggy-looking gentleman enter the forecastle with electronic equipment.

"Excuse me, is this the area where we can do the interviews?" David asked Boats. "Where should we setup the equipment?"

"Yes, sir," Boats replied. "Welcome to the forecastle onboard the newest carrier in the fleet. Let me give you guys the tour. This is where we house the anchor chain and two thrity-ton anchors that hold the massive carrier when anchored out . . ." As Boats gave them the tour, it was obvious that this area must have been a hotspot for tour routes. He acted as if he was teaching a school class going to the museum. Timmy smiled at Cindy, and they both giggled looking at Boats with his tour group.

The public affairs officer (PAO) had arranged some squadron sailors and ship's company to be interviewed about their jobs and national pride.

Timmy and Cindy, along with the rest of the company, was motioned by Boats to go to lunch. Everyone knew that this was going to be an easy day thanks to these civilian guests being entertained by Boats.

"Okay were almost ready," David said. "Who will we be interviewing first?"

Ah, we have an airman and a master chief ready," the PAO replied.

Caleigh briefed the airman on how to act on camera and be polite, speak loud. Billy double-checked all the audio equipment. His stomach was not getting any better.

"Okay, who wants to go first?" David asked again.

"Let the junior guys go first. I'm sure they will enjoy the spotlight." Master Chief he chuckled)

"Hey, Billy, you going to be okay?" Caleigh asked. "You don't look so good."

"I'll be fine," Billy replied. "I think I'm just seasick, I think. Go get them ready for the camera shots. I will be fine."

As the interview was about to begin, Caleigh signaled the "three, two, one, and action" with her fingers. All was going as planned. David smiled, explaining some of the facts, Boats told him earlier about the forecastle. The reporter now turned to the interview aspect of the story as the nervous sailor stood there. Caleigh gestured to smile as the sailor looked at her, and he relaxed. Her cute ways made even the most scared, camera-shy person feel less self-conscious. The intruption was now the sailor's eyes focused on the sound crew guy.

Billy, who was not looking well, could feel his stomach getting worse. "Are you okay?" Caleigh mouthed to Billy. He nodded he was fine, fighting the sickness. But then fell over on the equipment and started convulsing. David heard the crash and stopped the interview to see if Billy was okay. Everyone ran to check on him. Master Chief ran to the nearest phone and called medical to get to the forecastle. Blood and mucus was oozing out of his mouth. It was as if he was drowning in it. Boats remembered when he and his buddies would go on drinking binges. Boats ran over and put Billy on its side. The convulsion ceased.

Master Chief, in shock at all the blood on the floor, asked Boats, "Where did you learn that trick from?"

Boats smiled and said, "Keg parties, Master Chief."

It was about six or seven minutes, and medical was on scene. Caleigh, in tears, held Billy's hand as he tried to resist the urge to puke up more blood. His eyes were full of fear and doubt as he squeezed her hand. David, concerned for his friend, grabbed Caleigh away from Billy so the medical team can help him.

Boats told medical petty officers what happened. Billy's eyes were rolled in the back of his head. Non-responsive, he was strapped in the stretcher and was carried quickly to the medical department.

David and Caleigh tried to follow the medical team that hauled Billy to the ICU area but were told to go to their staterooms until a full diagnostics could be determined. After all the action that occurred and everyone left, Boats was looking at all the blood on the bulkheads and on the freshly painted deck, his hands covered in stained blood. This was a disaster. *Looks like 1st division is not going to like working late.* he thought to himself as he looked at his watch. "What a fucking mess. I'm sure Chief is going to say it's my fault," he said out loud.

"MAKE A HOLE!" the medical screamed as Billy was frantically rushed to the medical area. He was thrown on the surgery table as the medical personnel ripped his shirt, revealing Billy's skeleton drinker. The medical team scrambled to help him, and swung his arms for the medication to kick in. The constant heart monitor showed that his heartbeat was stable but fading. He looked more like a robot with IVs and wires keeping him alive. The ship's surgeon kept a close watch on him. The morphine kept him stable for now.

The doctor could not explain why he was having these bizarre symptoms. The brief with the commanding officer, the captain of the ship, ensured that he will be flown off the ship to a civilian hospital. Additional tests were going to be performed before he could be released.

The attention was now on David and Caleigh. Where were they prior to landing on the carrier? Were they in contact with anyone that was sick? Was this an unknown incident? The lie was all they had to stick with. Both denied everything. David did not want to lose his job, but Caleigh, feeling guilty on what just happened, was having doubts. They waited in their staterooms for Billy's results. Caleigh cried as she sat Indian style next to her bed.

David, sitting next to her, his hands covering his head, tried to calm Caleigh. "Hey, Caleigh, it will be fine. He will be fine."

"No, no, it will not be," Caleigh replied. "We have to tell them where we was! Maybe he was infected?"

"Are you serious? Listen to what you are saying? Infected with what? We all experienced the same thing. How come you and me didn't get sick?"

"I . . . I don't know, David!"

"Look you have to reason with me, Caleigh. He probably ain't used to the rocking of the ship, or maybe it was something he ate. We just need to sit tight until we are told otherwise. Don't fuck this up. We got out of that situation by the skin of our teeth and was given a second chance."

"I understand," Caleigh said as she calmed herself from crying. "I like him."

"I do too." He hugged her and kissed her head.

"No, I really like him, and not as a friend either."

"Oh, I didn't know . . . Well, hey, cheer up. Keep positive about this. I will think of something. He would not want you all hysterical. Please let's keep ourselves busy and watch the countless hours of footage that we have to edit to send back to the studio."

"Okay, you are right, David." Getting up from the floor, she grabbed the bag and sorted through the footage, trying to keep herself busy.

Blood transfusion was the only option for now. Much debate and argument were raging on how to treat Billy. Petty Officer Johnson, a hospital corpsman, was instructed by the doctors to hook up a simple blood bag containing 0+ blood. He wasn't going anywhere because of dehydration and massive loss of blood. Her experience in the medical field was like second nature. Billy lay there motionless. As the IV needle was inserted into his vein, blood was opened from the bag. It traveled from the IV bag around, filling the clear tube with blood. Looking at his tattoo on his chest, she smiled. "Must have been one hell of a party." As the blood reached his vein in his arm, something went terribly wrong. Petty Officer Johnson noticed his arm muscle spasm. His veins were dark purple, not normal for a man of his age. Like a tree root, his veins increased protruding near the surface of his skin.

His heart raced, Johnson leaned, over putting her hands on his chest to calm him. He was convulsing, blood filling all the whites in his eyes. It startled her seeing peaceful brown eyes fill with blood. "Oh my god, can I get some help in here please!" she screamed.

Billy screamed and groaned. She leaned over him to check the heart monitor, making sure she was reading it correctly. His eyes bulged as red blood filled around his eyes. Billy suddenly grabbed her hand. He held it, intrigued at her soft skin. It was as if he was having an out-of-body experience. Without thought, he bit the soft flesh that connects the index finger to the thumb. The sharp pain of teeth caught her by surprise, but it was too late. She had a chunk of flesh missing from her hand as the remains of blood dripped down his chin. Instinct kicked in, and she pulled back, making the wound worse. Holding her hand, she hid it from the other medical personnel that rushed into the room. Running out the room, she put water on it. The constant sting of the wound was unbearable pain. Her heartbeat throbbed in sync with the pain that ensued from the brief attack. After the blood stopped spewing, Johnson wrapped her injured hand in white gauze.

*It was a close call, but what would make a human bite another human?* Johnson thought. Her lie was that she cut herself on a surgical knife. "What happened to the man?" Johnson asked the nurse a moment later.

"He is in intensive care," the nurse replied. "The surgeon said he may be in a coma or something. He only reacts when he receives blood, but his body is rejecting the blood while at the same time his body craves for it. Blood tests were taken, and he will be flown off ASAP once we are near land. I'm sorry, Johnson. I know he was your patient."

"Yeah, I hope he is ok," Johnson said. "Let me know if you find out anything else. I can't believe he bit me."

"Johnson, are you okay? You don't look good. Did you get injured? I see you're holding your other hand wrapped in white gauze."

"Don't say anything. I will be okay. I just don't want to deal with paperwork. Hey, I am not feeling so good. I'm going to take some Motrin and eat something." She held her injured hand close to her chest and walked out the medical room.

. . . . .

Boats got some swabs and helped Cindy with the blood. The loud announcement of a medical emergency on the mess decks drowned the space. Boats grinned when every time the swab hit the deck, making a smooching sound of water and blood, he thought. *It was funny that she could not stand the sight of blood when she wanted to become a nurse.* Looking at his watch, he asked Cindy," You know where Timmy is? I told you both to get back here after chow." Cindy had that confused look on her face.

Timmy came running on the forecastle out of breath. He knew he was late, but he didn't care. "You guys would not believe what just happened on the mess decks," he said.

"I don't care," Boats said. "I want this mess cleaned up."

"Well, I want to know what happened," said Cindy.

"Oh my god, we was eating chow, and I know, I know. I was trying to finish because the lines were long as fuck. Anyways, Hospital Corpsman Johnson—you know the medical chick?"

"Yeah," Boats said. "We hung out with friends in England. What happened?"

"Well, I was sitting three tables away from her. She was just sitting there, staring at her food with her fork in her hand. I could tell something was wrong. The girl sitting next to her asked if she was okay. This girl tried to shake her, but Johnson wasn't moving. It was like she was frozen. There was a lot of busy talking about the blood on the forecastle. Anyways, it was creepy. I remember looking at her. It was like she wasn't there. I guess there was gauze wrapped around her hand from some injury. Then out of nowhere, this crazy bitch bit this crewmember on the arm. The chick screamed as a fucking chunk of her flesh was lying in someone's food. It caused such a commotion that everyone that was near her jumped up to get the hell away from her. It was fucking crazy. People were screaming, jumping over chairs and tables, all covered in blood. This green shirt guy, not paying attention, didn't notice that some of the flesh was in his soup, and he fucking ate it before I could warn him. I almost threw up when he swallowed it. Holy shit! Then Johnson threw up blood everywhere. When she threw up, I mean it had some pressure behind it. It got in their food, all over some people's faces, in their drinks. I know some idiot swallowed some blood. Three or four sailors got cut from her nails and teeth as they were trying to hold her down. By the time security got there, she already fucked up a few crewmembers. *Dude,* they had to knock her out to stop her from biting people. I got the fuck out of there as soon as they were making people help with the cleanup effort."

"Well, looks like we're not the only ones cleaning up a mess," Boats said. "Timmy, are you okay?"

"Yeah, I was not in the line of fire. But it was awesome! I have never seen anything more fucked up like that in my life."

. . . . .

"Did you hear that announcement, Caleigh?" David asked. "Something about security is needed on the mess decks. Fuck, this is bullshit. We're not going to sit in this room forever. I need to talk to someone about what's going on with Billy."

"Hey, calm down," Caleigh said, "We're on a military ship. It's their call. And besides, wasn't it you to tell me to wait?"

"Screw this. Grab the cam. We're going to find out what the hell is going on."

. . . . .

Master Chief walked through medical area. "Excuse me, I have an appointment with the doctor," he said to the young female receptionist. She smiled and told him to have a seat. How long will he have to wait? He grew impatient but knew how procedures went. He decided to have small talk with her. "How is the patient doing?"

"Huh? The one that was brought in? The civilian guy?" Her frown soon got sober then told him the news that he probably won't make it.

A loud crash was heard that got her attention. Master Chief asked, "What was that?"

"Oh, its nothing," she said. "Maybe the ship is rocking, and some stuff wasn't secured properly for sea. I will check it out."

It was the same room where Billy was in. The young woman walked in and noticed that the body was missing. Blood spatters were all over the white sheets, and it looked like a tornado hit the place. Stuff was everywhere. *Jesus Christ, what a mess,* she thought to herself. Then the soft groan coming from the closet caught her attention. "Hello, is anyone there!" she shouted. "Guys, I know I'm the new girl from Georgia, but if this is a prank, I'm not impressed." The soft voice of growls was getting louder as she approached the medical closet. Cautiously, she opened the door. Billy was standing there. Blood oozed out his eyes, his skin was dark, and there purple bruise marks on him where there were IVs once. Limping in his hospital gown, he reached out to her. Before she could react, he grabbed her by the hair. He was clearly stronger than this five-foot African American ebony woman. Her reaction was a loud scream.

Master Chief heard the scream from the waiting room. Jumping up, he knew something was wrong. Walking down the hall, he noticed blood smear marks on the circular glass windows. It was as if a hand was trying to get out. His cautious walk prepared him for anything behind the two swinging doors. Slowly easing the door open, he announced his name. The grunt and moans could be heard behind the hospital bed. Easing with his fists ready, he saw the blood on the bedsheets. "Hello, are you okay? Is anyone in here?" Master Chief said. He could hear the rustle of something behind the table. As he slowly eased over, he saw the horrific sight. "What the fuck!" he said out loud.

Billy was no more the once-caring human. He gorged on the young woman's flesh. Ripping open her chest, she just lay there not moving. The eerie sound of her flesh grinding in his mouth was a new sound Master Chief never heard before. "Hey, what the hell do you think you are doing?" Master Chief shouted at him. The heartless human ignored him as blood dripped down his chin. Then it just stopped feeding. This thing slowly stood up, and now his attention was on Master Chief. It snarled and spit blood, eyes bloodshot, his hands and forearms drenched in blood. Master Chief backed up and tried to reason with it. It was not listening to anything. His vision could see the pulsing glow of blood running through Master Chief's body. There it was—he could see the orange glow of Master Chief's heart as it pulsed faster and faster. It was like a high to him. His vision was like that of infrared, seeing the heart.

"Hey, sir, don't do it. I'm warning you, if you come any closer, I will defend myself," he said with a stern voice. Without hesitation, it lunged at him. But it was not expecting a fast retaliation. Master Chief Spartan-kicked it right in the chest. The hit was so hard, the creature flew back and fell behind the hospital bed. It tried to balance itself but ended up taking everything down with him. The loud shatter of surgical tools and hospital pans made a loud bang as everything fell to the floor. From the right corner of his eye, Master Chief could see the unrecognizable figure of the woman that was lying on the floor. Her chest and organs seeping out of the chunk marks left by her murderer.

Her once-beautiful hair was now soaked in blood. Now tried to stand up, and she wanted a piece of Master Chief as well. She ran toward him, and he grabbed the chair by the back and swung it like a bat right at her. She fell to the left of him and lay there. Billy was now getting back up from his first encounter. Master Chief had a look of confusion and backed away. The grunting and growling made the hair stand up on his neck. These things wanted to kill Master Chief. Backing towards the wall, he realized he was trapped. The exit door was more like a gauntlet. Master Chief thought of how he was going to get out of this alive but was soon interrupted by the two infected creatures, both getting up and facing him. "You have got to be fucking kidding me," he said as he cracked his knuckles.

. . . . .

Katy Perry's "Teenage Dream" blared out of an iPod hooked up to the helicopter's speakers. Lieutenant Jenny McCormick circled about three thousand feet around the aircraft carrier. She smiled with her female co-pilot, and the helicopter felt like it was her second home. Three other guys were in the back with the door open, guns sticking out the sides. She could see people hurrying about the decks, preparing for her refueling. "I love my fucking job!" She smiled. On the ship's radio, she was instructed to land near the forward side of the flight deck on the port side. The yellow-shirted crewmember on the flight deck signaled for her return.

As she came around for a second pass, a call came in to halt all aircrafts. The skipper was grounding everyone. "Hey, what the hell is going on?" Jenny had concern on her face. This was not normal. She controlled the tail for the landing, and it was as smooth as before. Doing her last-minute shut-off checks, Jenny would not leave until the propellers stopped rotating. "Hey, Lieutenant, XO wants to have an all-hands muster in the hangar bay. It must be important," a sailor said to Jenny. Looking at her watch, she followed him, "Damn it, no dinner tonight."

It was about 7:00 pm or 1900 hours, military time, when the entire ship's crew assembled in the hangar bay. Boats and Timmy were both annoyed because of the fact they that had the mid-watch and will be lacking sleep. The massive carrier held three huge hangar bays, but it was Hangar Bay II that the stage and speakers were set up. Over four thousand personnel and sailors stood in ranks, waiting for the executive officer (XO) to show.

"Attention on deck!" the master-at-arms shouted.

Everyone was silent at attention. When the second in command executive officer, spoke, it was addressed to the entire crew of the aircraft carrier. He walked on a platform that was about three feet high from the ground so he can see everyone. There was enough personnel to fill the entire hangar bay area.

"As as you were, everyone," the XO began. "I have been briefed on the situation at hand with this incident on the chow mess decks earlier today. I can assure you that any personnel that was in direct contact is in the care of medical as we speak. The commanding officer did not want to have this all-hands meeting. He and many of the department heads felt it was a bad idea having so many sailors in one area. This was my call, shipmates, not his. The commanding officer is on a video conference with the Pentagon from Washington DC. The medical tests were sent there for further investigation, and it was of great interest for the United States that we remain at sea until told otherwise. Currently, we are two hundred miles from the nearest unknown land. The Orders from Washington DC, we have been directed not to go into port. This is very serious, so I need everyone to listen up and pay attention. We could be dealing with a possible virus. I assure you, it is not to get alarmed about. We will go on our daily business."

People started talking and muttering in the crowd.

The XO went on, "If anyone else feels that you need to get tested or you came in contact with *the incident* that occurred on the mess decks, please go to medical. This is extremely serious. We don't know exactly what we are dealing with here. The ship's medical officer has informed me that we just need to keep record of those who have been exposed so we can treat them immediately. If you have any of the following symptoms, please report to medical immediately. The symptoms are as follows . . ."

As this was going on, the ship's masters-at-arms were patrolling the aft hangar bay. It was there that they noticed an aviation boatswain mate third class in a green shirt and dark navy blue flight deck pants facing the bulkhead. His back toward them, this guy just stood there. He had his left shoulder slouched down with his head facing the floor.

They were walking together, talking about vacation and what they were going to do once they get new orders. "Hey, look. What's he doing?" one of them said as he pointed at a lone green-shirt sailor facing the wall.

"Not sure, let's go have some fun," the other guy said acting as if he was going to grab his baton.

"Hey, shipmate," the first master-at-arms said. "Aren't you supposed to be in Hangar Bay II? Excuse me, I am talking to you."

"Hey, man, leave him alone," said the second master-at-arms. "He isn't bothering anyone."

"No, XO said all hands, so he is no exception." As the first master-at-arms approached the sailor, he kept his left hand on his baton. "Hey, shipmate," he continued, "I'm talking to you! Do you hear me?" He reached over and grabbed his arm. Swinging him around. The expression on his face was enough to make his partner's hair stand up on his neck. A mix of blood and saliva dripped from his bottom lip. The obvious blood stain on his chest was either from his own doing or another sailor he possibly attacked. "HOLY SHIT WHAT THE HELL ARE YOU? HOLY SHIT! HOLY SHIT!" the master-at-arms screamed and tried to draw his gun.

This thing did not hesitate as it went for his face. It ended up biting a chunk out of his right cheek. You could hear the crunch of his cheekbone as it gnawed through his flesh, and then he found the major artery in his neck. Blood spewed everywhere. His tongue ran up and down the master-at-arm's face, licking up the leaking blood like a crazy man on crack.

His partner was in shock as he saw his friend lay on the ground, taking his last breath. Gasping for air, he was holding the wound in his neck. The infected walker stood up. His eyes bloody, his face purple, veins bulging from the feeding. Blood dripped where he walked. The master-at-arms fled in so much panic. He ran toward the crowd that was listening to the executive officer. In hot pursuit, the walker now became a runner, his hands swinging as he ran toward the people. His eyes saw so many veins and heartbeats.

"Everybody, RUN! GET OUT OF HERE! This thing killed my partner! EVERYONE, GET THE FUCK OUT OF HERE!" the frantic master-at-arms screamed. Everyone looked in the direction and saw him running toward them. He got within ten feet of the crowd, turned around, and drew his gun. He pointed it at the creature, but just as he was about to fire, another sailor grabbed his gun and made him shoot up in the air. This sailor thought he was doing the right thing, not seeing what the patrolman was so afraid of. As the fellow crew member restrained him and announced his name, "I am AO1 Nicholson, and you need to calm the fuck down!" Another Petty officer yelled at the patrolman saying . . ."Are you crazy? He is not armed!" the sailor said as he kicked the gun away from his reach. Others took the master-at-arms to the ground and restrained him.

"NO, YOU ARE MAKING A BIG MISTAKE! GET THE FUCK OFF OF ME! LOOK AT HIM! HE IS ARMED WITH THE INFECTION!"

A few other sailors got involved holding him down.

"Oh my god, we are all going to die," he said as his face was pressed between the nonskid and a sailor's knee. That very instant, the infected sprinted and leaped ten feet right into the unsuspecting crowd. Petty Officer Nicholson stood there frozen, realizing what a terrible mistake he made. The infected began slashing, biting, attacking anyone within his reach. Confusion was everywhere as people were screaming, trying to get away. It sounded like a stadium of people screaming at a football game. The XO tried to calm things, but now there were more people were infected and were turning. The initial attack made some of the victims convulse. Holding their head they screamed in so much pain as blood rushed in their eyes. No more did they have pupils. Replaced by white growth and blood they could see no more.

Blood was everywhere. In the mouth were organs and intestines. People were in agony as they were randomly bit or scratched, and that sealed their fate. Those who got away ran for their lives. In the fleeing crowd, Boats, Timmy, and a handful crewmembers were just trying to leave the infected area. Boats headed to the forecastle as others followed him. Timmy held on to Cindy's hand and pulled her. In the mass confusion, an infected crewmember hit Cindy, knocking her to the ground. Her hand was ripped away from Timmy who got pushed with the crowd. He could not find her as he cried her name. Timmy tried to go back, but the mob was pushing Timmy farther and farther away from her.

"Cindy?" Timmy shouted, "Where are you? Cindy?"

"No time, Timmy!" Boats said. "Get the fuck out of here, or you will end up like that!"

Only five feet away, a crewmember was tackled by one of the already infected, had its arm bitten, and soon another joined, biting his fingers off. These fuckers were viscous.

The crowd was pushing and shoving, and Cindy, now trampled, got back on her feet and followed the confused mob. Jenny was also involved in the disaster scene, running frantically to get out of the hangar bay. The sound of an M16 firing went off as retaliation of so many already infected. At first only warning shots were fired to calm the mob, but it only made things worse. The security team did not know how to take them down. Hitting them in the leg or in the chest with batons and spraying them with OC spray did little to calm the crowd, but still they charged, more pissed off than before. Instantly, once the infection happened, they changed. Bullets making deep-impact wounds on the walking corpses did not stop their hunger for blood.

One of the infected stood up looking at the patrolman after he got his arm torn to shreds. Slowly walking towards the scared guy, his walk evolved into a sprint. The security guard pointed the M-16 and fired. The impact pushed him on his back as three bullets pierced his chest. As the patrolman lowered his weapon, he dropped his guard for a second checking his rounds. The creature did a sit up and bit the patrolman's leg.

Hundreds of them were dead but were still walking. One witnessed a patrolman pumping about fifteen to twenty rounds in the dead man's chest, but he still charged.

Crewmembers were attacking each other as many were soaked in blood. Some female officer got her hair pulled, and she was dragged into the corner where others joined and attacked her.

Many were witnesses as the infection got out of control. As fast as it entered your body, you were one of them.

Boats had about twenty survivors locked up on the forecastle. This was the area where the anchor chains were stowed. Included in the group was Timmy, a religious sailor named Petty Officer Smith and some other shipmates from the deck department, a few gunners, and engineer personnel. Timmy was upset from getting separated from Cindy. His concern would test Boats in this hairy situation.

"Everyone, quiet down. As long as these two hatches remain shut, there is no way they can get in," Boats said.

People were crying and praying to the Lord for forgiveness. Boats didn't want to hear it. With a scared grin, he looked at Timmy and said, "What the fuck was that? What the hell happened?"

Timmy tried to wipe the tears from his face. Shaking his head, he said," I don't know. I saw them pump bullets in them, and they still charged as if it didn't bother them."

"How many we got in here?" Boats asked. "Twenty shipmates? Keep them fucking doors dogged shut tight and make sure no one gets in. I don't want to clean up this blood again."

Timmy looked at Boats with a shocked look on his face. Pointing at his navy blue coveralls, he said in a scared voice, "You're already covered in blood."

# Chapter 4

*QUARANTINED*

David and Caleigh were running into the direction that everyone was fleeing from. There was so much panic and crying. Every other person had injuries either from the attack or from the mob trying to flee the area. "What the hell is going on!" David said, looking at the frantic people running away from something. Caleigh was right behind him, rolling the camera. Everything was being recorded. Pushing and shoving were all that could be seen through the lens while they went through the small passageways. Confusion was everywhere. David held on to Caleigh's hand, trying to push through the crowd. They were located on the 03 level, about three decks above the main hangar bay. People warned him not to enter the hangar bay. But all this excitement was what he was looking for. Working his way down to the 02 deck, the crowds were less and less. "One more deck to go, Caleigh. You okay?" he said checking on her. He could see her shaking as there were blood marks all over the freshly painted white walls.

They quietly eased their way down the metal ladder from the 01 level to one of the main entrances leading to the hangar bay doors when they noticed people on the ground. There were three of them on all fours, looking at something about two feet from the ground. "Hey, you guys okay?"David said as he shined his flashlight on them. They were hiding in a dark area. One of them looked up with blood spewing from its mouth. The infected hissed and growled at them when he noticed the vision of fresh veins and a rapid heartbeat. The other two looked up, mimicking the first one. When they got up, they moved toward the ladder. And Caleigh saw what they were doing on the floor. They were feeding on another human casualty. The victim had its arm dislocated along with his neck completely ripped opened, and its liver and kidneys ripped out. The infected was holding its victim's kidneys in his hand, sucking out the blood like it was a Capri Sun drink.

"David, I think we should go back up. David? Let's go now!" Caleigh screamed, crying as they slowly backed away going up the ladder well. David held on to the rails with two hands and kicked with his two legs as one of them that was trying to come up the stairs. The domino effect knocked all three of them down. When the creatures got up, both David and Caleigh were gone.

Cindy ended up one deck below the hangar bay, near the aft mess decks. About three hundred sailors, men and women, were with her. They closed every door that could lead into the mess decks, and they reinforced them immediately. The door on the port side where the speed chow line would begin was almost breached as twenty of them tried to get through, strewing their infected blood everywhere.

The constant banging and scratching on the metal hatch drove any human insane afraid beyond what he could bear. Cindy could see three sailors holding down the handlebar as the dead were trying to pry it up. A chief was screaming, trying to take control of the situation. He was trying to survive like everyone else was. His voice cracked with fear. Emergency generators kicked on reserve power. "Shit, they got to the electric power supply!" the chief screamed.

Another petty officer walked by. "No, I don't think they did anything to the power. They probably got attacked. They probably hit the power in the process."

As if the commotion weren't enough of a threat, now the red lights limited their vision. The white lights that lit everything up now gleamed a red haze reflected everywhere. Cindy sat on the chair where food was once served. Makeup dripped down her face from her tears. Clearly she wore too much. As order and discipline was forming, the captain came over the loud speaker. "Crewmembers, carrier air wing, and officers, this is the captain. Shipmates, I was just informed of the attack that occurred in the hangar bay earlier. It was against my discretion to order all hands to muster. It was the executive officer's decision, and it was a fatal mistake. In the commotion of it, all the XO was attacked and is infected. I am issuing a full quarantine of the entire ship. All hands are to remain in their berthing and offices. All doors will be boarded up. All hatches will be secured. I am ordering an immediate lockdown for all hands until we can control the situation. If you are approached by an infected person, do not engage. We don't know exactly how this virus spreads. The only personnel allowed to roam freely will be the security force. They will take every effort to take back the ship. We will be getting assistance from other U.S. Navy ships that will enforce our protection and ensure this outbreak stays here and does not leave this ship. Security is guarding my door as we speak. Please if you are infected, contact security, and they will help you. If you know anyone that is infected, avoid them at all costs. Contact with them may only put fellow shipmates in danger. Please remain calm, and this will be over soon. Thank you and may God bless us all. That is all."

After the captain made his announcement, everyone was quiet. The shock of this reality was finally bestowed upon the remaining survivors of the crew. Cindy stayed in her seat with her knees folded up by her face, her hideaway spot as she silently cried and hoped that Timmy was okay. The dark red lights made it hard to see. Her hair, no longer up in a military standard, now hung down in her eyes. Wiping her tears, she smeared her makeup all over her face and down her neck. She could hear people's concern over everything that was going on. More people filtered into the mess decks. Cindy had counted over three hundred personnel and was estimating how much food would last if this took days, weeks, or maybe months. "Shipmate, can you help out the injured?" said an officer.

She nodded and headed over those who got injured by getting trampled fleeing from the hangar bay.

. . . . .

"Okay, so we really don't know what we are dealing with here," Boats said.

"Yeah, we do," Timmy replied. "I *saw* them fucking unload entire clips in them, and still they charged."

"I bet they missed," Boats countered. "I'm sure they were not even hitting them."

"Dude, are you serious right now? The security force was at point-blank range. It still went after him. These fucking things are dead."

"What? Are you listening to what you are saying? We are not dealing with that! Hell no."

"Hey, I know what the fuck I saw! Those things ain't alive no more. No human can stand entire clips of ammo being pumped in its chest and still try to attack."

Boats and Timmy grabbed any gear that could be used as a weapon. They were now about twenty strong, and this was a good-sized guard force if they were breached. Boats really wasn't that concerned because the forecastle had only two ways in that were secured shut. A second class petty officer stood up. His name tag said Smith, and he and wanted to pray with everyone. Pulling a Bible from his back pocket, his hands were shaking as he was trying to find the right passage. Most people huddled in a circle and joined in. When Boats was invited in the worried group, he shook his head and was acting as if he was busy checking any possible makeshift weapons.

"Hey, Boats, you think you're better than us, huh?" Smith said.

"No," Boats replied. "I just rather keep my opinions to myself."

"Well, looks like all we have is time, so why don't you enlighten us?" Smith said.

"I am not religious," Boats replied. "I respect your views and opinions, but I rather keep busy. There is much to do if those things try to breach through the doors."

"Well, if you don't believe in something, then where do you think you go in the next life? I will tell you where you will go, to hell."

"If you are so sure, then leave. Why survive if you know you will go to paradise? Last time I checked, hell is right outside that *fucking* door." Boats pointed to the door.

"Do not mock God! We are all God's children. I know my faith. It says in the gospel of John—"

In an instant, Boats ran up to Smith and grabbed him by the collar and yelled at him, with the intent to threaten him. "DON'T THROW YOUR RELIGION ON ME, SHIPMATE! YOU ALL WANT TO PRAY? GO AHEAD! I HAVE ENOUGH OF OTHER SHIT TO WORRY ABOUT THAN SCRIPTURES. YOU THINK PRAYER IS GOING TO STOP THEM FROM RIPPING OUT YOUR FUCKING HEART?"

Silence grew in the room then was replaced by the repeated banging on the port door.

"I think . . . they are here!" Timmy said.

It was a slow banging at first, then increased. The moans and cries of the dead wanted in. They could hear the argument within the forecastle.

Boats just looked at Smith as if he was going to punch him. Smith knew he better shut up before he made things worse. Boats and Timmy ran to the door to make sure the chains were secured in order to prevent the handle from being lifted.

"Seems like they are just banging," Timmy said. "I don't think they know how to open it."

"Just how long do you think we can stay up in here?" Boats said. "We have no food. And the water fountain is outside. Here, take this pry bar and wedge it tight against the door. I will post a watch just to be sure they don't enter. We will rotate everyone."

. . . . .

Cindy helped carry water as she was ordered by the officer. This would make the time go by. Located on the mess decks, all entrances were blocked off. Looking in the corner, Cindy saw two crewmember officers holding wounds. She went over to them and spoke, "Hey, are you both okay? What are your names?"

"I will be okay," replied one of them. "I'm Ensign Perez. This is Lieutenant Logan."

"Nice to meet you, ma'am," Cindy said. "Can I look at that?"

"Sure, it's pretty nasty, Perez replied. "One of them scratched me and the lieutenant. His is much worse than mine."

"Oh, let me get the security guys. They will be able to help you."

"Thank you. I didn't want to be a problem."

Cindy got up and grabbed one of the security guys who were checking his ammo. He walked over to where Perez was lying. "Hey, did you get scratched or bitten?" he asked. She nodded her head yes as she revealed the bleeding wound. He then turned his back to confirm what to do on the radio. Cindy smiled, giving her the okay signal. Perez smiled, giving a faint thumbs-up. Everything was going to be all right.

Without hesitation, the security patrolman turned around with his 9MM drawn and said, "Ma'am, I am sorry. May God have mercy on your soul!" He shot her in the head. The loud bang made a few people duck. Cindy stood there in shock, screaming as the close-range kill sent blood spewing all over her face. The security patrolman confirmed, "Look, I am just doing what I am told. All infected personnel must be put down in order to control whatever this is!"

Everyone was in shock. No one moved as he put his gun back in his holster. "Didn't you say there were two of them?" he asked Cindy. Cindy stepped back, looking at him as if the grim reaper was standing right behind him. A sound of soft breathing slowly increased as he turned around. There stood the lieutenant, blood dripping from his mouth, his eyes pure white with blood seeping from them.

The security patrolman saw everyone in front of him back up. The hairs stood up on the back of his neck. When he turned around, it turned his head sideways and bit his neck, ripping this throat right out. Blood went everywhere as this demon feasted. Cindy hid under the tables. She knew the infection was there. The poor sailors beat him, trying to get him off the guard, but no one bothered to grab his gun. The cold creature stood up and lunged on its next victim. Soon the guard stumbled to his feet, ready to attack the next victim. Panic now ensued. They were so sure to keep those out, but they could not escape. They created their own grave. Cindy stayed quiet and not moving, covering her ears to ignore the attacks and the agony of bloodcurdling cries of help.

. . . . .

Boarding themselves in an office on the 03 level, which is three decks above the main hangar bay, David and Caleigh sat and waited. His back was against the door as he heard people running outside, trying to get safe. Often he could hear someone getting attacked while others tried to outrun them. The grunting and heavy footsteps of the walkers were different than the living.

"What are we going to do?" Caleigh asked.

"Well, let's look at our options," David replied. "We're surrounded by water. There is no real place we can go. We're somewhere in the ocean. Didn't you ever see *Cast Away* with Tom Hanks?"

"But that would be better than here."

She put her hand over her face as she cried in panic. David just crouched, not knowing what to say. Frustrated, he banged the back of his head on the door. Soon he heard another bang. Caleigh looked up. David knocked three times. The knock repeated three times.

"Oh my god! Hello, are you okay? Hello?" David asked the person behind the door.

The tiny voice answered, "Hey, I'm Lieutenant Jenny McCormick. I am a helicopter pilot. Are you guys okay?"

"Holy shit!" Caleigh exclaimed. "This is our ticket out of here."

"I am in the room next to you," Jenny said. "What the hell is going on?"

"We are not sure," David replied. "People are getting sick. I am David and I am here with my co-worker Caleigh. We are both civilians, reporters."

"Oh, do you have a cell phone?" Jenny asked.

"Yes," said David. "But we cannot get a signal."

"Yes, you can," Jenny said. "Uh, I mean we have to get to the bridge. I know the outside codes to call out of here. There is no way were going to make it there with all them everywhere."

"Then we will wait a few," David suggested. "They are active now. Not a good idea to go anywhere now. "

"So you are a pilot?" Caleigh asked.

Yes, I am, but getting to the plane is not going to be easy. Get some sleep. We cannot go anywhere now. We will wait until morning."

"Okay, Jenny," David said. "I will set my alarm. Are you going to be okay?"

"Yeah, my leg is wedged against the door. See you all in the morning."

"Yeah, if we make it that far," Caleigh said.

David hit Caleigh in the arm. "Shut up. What the hell are you doing? Don't scare her. She is our only way out of here."

Caleigh held her head in shame and grabbed some blankets to sleep. Tomorrow will be a long day.

· · · · ·

Cindy lay often listening to them scurry by. So many have been killed and infected. She saw someone trying to run away. His arm knocked over the ketchup bottle off on the table, and instantly they swarmed him.

Cindy feared she could not stay there forever. Once everyone changed, they would eventually hunt her. So crawling out from under the table, she was going to make a run for it. Crouching in a sprint position, she could see them feasting. But just as she was going to take off, a big hand grabbed her from around her mouth.

She figured the infected had her. She struggled screaming, kicking, and swinging—until it spoke. "Shhhhhhh! They follow noise. Shut the fuck up, or I will choke you out. Watch and don't make fucking sound." Picking up a napkin holder, the man threw it across the room. When it hit the wall, a loud bang echoed as the horde charged toward the noise. The whispering voice spoke in her ear, "I am sorry to scare you. Please don't be afraid. It's Master Chief."

# Chapter 5

## *THE PLAN*

2:00 am and the loud shrill of shrieks woke Timmy up. All he could think about was Cindy, wondering if she was one of them or if she escaped. Rubbing his eyes, he felt his back hurt from lying on the cold floor. He got up and saw Boats working. On a blanket, he saw tools laid out. No one could sleep as often crewmembers begged to be let in, crying as they were attacked at the door. They were not allowed in because of the rate of how fast the infection spread.

Two sledgehammers, a couple of thee-foot marlinespikes, some five-foot-long pry bars. Daniel, one of the boatswain mate petty officers, was helping Boats get out these tools. Timmy spoke, "Damn, Boats, you act like we're going to drop the anchor." Boats didn't say a word. Going behind the curtain where line 4 would have led out the chalk if they were pier side, Timmy saw three or four broken mop handles. The ends were carved into spears, and some had sharp tools attached to them like some medieval weapon.

"Some time before the sun set last night, I opened up the chalk and saw we're not alone out here," Boats said. "There are CGs and DDGS. Saw thee FFGs surrounding us. Makes me wonder if we are quarantined. The goddamn fleet is here. They know something is up. I figured we can get to the life rafts or maybe the RHIB (which was known as rigged hull inflatable boat.). It's the only way we can get out of here."

"So you and Danny are going to leave?" Timmy asked.

"No, only a few of us are going," Danny replied. "We will either drop the RHIB or life raft, and you will stay here and tie some line to the bits and throw it out the chock opening to the water, make a line so they can climb down. We've been dead in the water for some time now."

"Okay, sounds like a plan," Timmy said.

"Does anyone know what we are dealing with?" Boats replied.

"Not really," Timmy replied, "but I think it's best we don't come in contact with them."

"Look," Boats said, "we will have to defend ourselves. I am clueless as to what we are dealing with out those doors."

"We will have to pay close attention," Timmy replied. "I mean if I saw the security guys unloading entire clips in the ones infected and they still charged, they may be harder than we estimated to avoid."

"Are there different types?" Danny asked.

"I am not the expert dealing with these things," Timmy replied. "I told you I have no idea what they even are, if they are even human anymore."

"They have been at it all night, Boats said. "Eating, feasting, hunting, infecting others. I think they are acute in hearing. I heard them enter the berthing area on the other side. I don't think anyone made it. We will need to cause a distraction. Everyone, get some sleep. You will need it. Tomorrow we're out of here."

. . . . .

On 0700, the soft beep on Jenny's watch woke her up. Her neck was stiff from sleeping next to the door. She was too scared to sleep in the bed the fear of getting attacked in her sleep. Cracking her door, she was very quiet to see what was going on outside. Her eye scanned as she saw nothing, only ghostly smears of blood along the walls and floors. Peeking a little bit more, she saw that around ten was standing there about twenty-five feet down the passageway. She got startled and shut her door. "Fuck, they are still there," she said. She heard three knocks from the other room.

"Hey, was that you that opened the door?" David asked.

Jenny told them what she saw.

We're trapped," Caleigh said. "How are we going to get out of here?"

"I am not sure," Jenny replied. "I am working on that. Do you have any weapons? We cannot leave without defending ourselves."

"Let me look," David said. "Caleigh, check the bathroom."

As the two of them hurried to see if there was anything they could use, Jenny did the same. She had a pocketknife her father gave her when she joined the navy. "This will have to do," she said. She duct-taped it to a broom handle, and it was now a deadly weapon. Caleigh found a piece of iron, best thing she could come up with. David got a hold of his belt. The buckle could be used as a weapon, not a very effective one, but it will have to do.

"Hey, Jenny, how many are out there?" David asked.

"Uh, I saw about ten of them, but there could be more," Jenny replied. "They are twenty-five feet away, just walking in circles, bumping into each other. Once you open the door, they are to the right of you. The left side looked clear."

David opened his door quietly and verified they were still there. He was afraid that if he made a run for it, others could be waiting for him in the next corner. He crept out, moving away from them. Caleigh soon followed, and Jenny was right behind them. It was too easy, he thought to himself. As they started getting some distance, Caleigh never shut the door completely, and the roll of the ship closed the door hard. Everyone froze as the noise got the zombies' attention. "SHIT, RUN! EVERYONE, RUN!" Jenny cried. The horde was awake, running after them in a full sprint. Blood spewed from their mouths. Screams soon attracted more to the action in the long passageway. David found a door to the right, and they ran. Once Jenny got through, they shut the door, severing some of zombies' fingers in the door. They pushed the handle all the way down, and the fingers fell.

The constant pounding on the door soon pissed them off.

"Hey, David, we're outside. I don't know where," Caleigh said.

"We are on the catwalks," Jenny told them. "Oh my god, look, we're surrounded!" She pointed at the ocean, the American navy surrounded the carrier. About ten ships total kept their distance about five miles away. Helicopters and fighter jets flew overhead. The loud roar of the jets made everyone cover their ears. Jenny then walked up the small ladder well leading to the flight deck. She got halfway when she ran back down as if something startled her.

"What is it? Why are you stopping?" David asked.

"They are everywhere, all over the flight deck, the dead ones," Jenny replied. "I guess the jets are attracting them. There has to be hundreds of them. Shit, we need another plan."

Hiding on the aft port side catwalk, the three of them hid under the ladder well, staying quiet and trying to devise a plan.

. . . . .

Master Chief kept quiet as the cursed was in the other room eating. He grabbed some guns from the fallen guards and checked their ammo. He had a 9MM pistol and three full clips, and he made sure there was one in the chamber. The slide of the clicking noise woke up Cindy. His finger over his lips was his way of saying, "Keep quiet. They are still here."

She whispered, "Hey, did you sleep?"

"No," Master Chief replied. "I had to make sure we didn't encounter the smart ones."

"Smart ones?"

After I encountered the first ones in the hospital, when the initial outbreak happened in the hangar bay, these smart ones, I watched them avoid the guns, check doors, wait. I think I know which ones are the smart ones."

Which ones? I don't understand."

"Well, I think that, in theory, if you have a high IQ when you were alive, then you will enhance that for survival mode once you're infected. We have to be careful of the reactor sailors that got infected. I saw them wait as the patrolman unloaded in this one infected crewmember, and when the guy emptied his clip, they attacked. They are going to be the biggest threat. We can tell them apart because they should be wearing TLD badges on them. All reactor sailors got them. They were issued to reactor crewmembers to detect radiation areas. So if you see a TLD, run." Said master chief.

"Kind of makes you wonder what else got enhanced. I mean all the weight lifters and then the athletes."

"Well, I don't want to stick around and find out. We need to get to the armory. There are plenty of guns, ammo. We can even the odds."

"Can't we find the guards?"

""Are you crazy? Did you not see that one guy waste that female officer? They can't be trusted. They are only following orders. Shhhh, stay down!"

There were three of them walking from the right side. One was smelling around, and the other two were following. They grunted, and blood spewing from their mouths made spattering sounds on the polished floor. One of them bent forward listening to the blood hit the deck. Licking it with his tongue, he looked under the table. Staring for a few seconds, it howled and walked away. Cindy stopped holding her breath as Master Chief wiped his face from sweat. "That was close," he said. Instantly the table they hid under was flipped over. Master Chief stared at the creature's TLD badge. The creature looked at what he was staring at and ripped off his TLD badge, holding it in his clawlike hand and threw threw at Master Chief. Cindy grabbed Master Chief's gun and pointed it at the smart one, firing it directly into his heart, and it got pushed back. "Are you fucking stupid? You just called the dinner bell!" Master screamed as he grabbed the gun from Cindy.

"I'm sorry I thought—" Cindy began.

"Here, this way run!" Master Chief bellowed.

They jumped on the tables. It was now or never. The horde will soon follow. The smart one followed but kept his distance. Cindy was right behind Master Chief. The smart one lunged into Master Chief's back, trying to bite him. Master Chief already saw him and reached from behind and grabbed the smart one by its exposed flesh and threw him off. He hit the soda machines with such force it was hesitant getting up.

"You may be smart, but you are not strong," Master Chief said.

"He may not be strong, but they are!" Cindy pointed at the horde. "RUN!"

About thirty of them came running at them. Master Chief grabbed Cindy's hand and pulled her. Opening the sealed door, he hoped there were not more on the other side. Without checking, they busted through. There was only one, and the 9MM took him out with a quick headshot.

"One more door and we go down a ladder well to the right!" Master Chief said. "Whatever you see, don't stop."

She nodded in terror. As the door opened, another fifteen of them were waiting for them. Master Chief fired a couple of shots and ran down the ladder well. Cindy was right behind him. One of them grabbed her hair, pulling and dragging her up the ladder. Master Chief tried to help, but there were too many of them. There was nothing he could do. Running back down, he was able to close the hatch since they were distracted with Cindy. He could hear the mauling through the top. It made him feel bad. How could he let her die? Making his way, he called out, "Hello, is anyone down here?" There was no answer, but a noise caught his attention. Slowly creeping around the corner, he saw one of them scratching and trying to get inside the door. He was trying to get something. Master Chief whistled. "Hey, fuck face, over here!" As it turned, Master Chief drilled two bullets in its head. The blood splatter exited from its head on to the wall. The footsteps of another crept from behind lockers. One clear shot in its head sent him to fall to his knees then flat on its face.

"Hey, are you alive?" Master Chief asked through the door. "Answer me. If you do not answer, I will come in blazing guns!"

Opening the door, Master Chief discovered that it was a small room. Two zombies banging on the bars turned to Master Chief, and three shots took them out. Looking behind the bars, Master Chief could see survivors, two of them holding on their guns. "Open up! I am not one of them. If I was, I would not be talking to you," he said catching his breath. They shook their heads no. "OPEN THE FUCKING DOOR! I AM A MASTER CHIEF!" he screamed at them. They immediately jumped up and opened the door. "Sorry, I know you are just following orders," Master Chief said. "I hate pulling my rank like that, guys."

The young man stood up. "I am Gunner's Mate Third Class Mark Winston. This is Quartermaster Third Class Andrew Barich." Andrew was a tall fellow. His California beach-bum look and blonde hair made him stand out in a crowd.

Shaking Master Chief's hand, he spoke, "I got caught up in all the confusion, been here ever since the hangar bay incident."

"What kind of guns do you have?" Master Chief asked.

"We got 9mms, M16s, also got 12-gauge shotgun pump action, and for the bad asses, the M240 automatic," Winston replied.

"Does anyone know what happened?" Master Chief asked. "What is the plan?"

"Well, we don't really have a plan. Just kind of playing it by ear," Andrew said.

Just as the conversation started, the loud speaker was turned on. "Everyone onboard, this is the captain. If there is anyone left, do what you have to do to survive. We have been informed that we are in a quarantine status. If we attempt to leave the ship, deadly force will be enforced by the surrounding ships. They understand the situation and have been given orders to keep this situation contained as much as possible."

A loud banging could be heard in the background as if some of them were attempting to get inside his room. His door was made of wood as most important officers doors were. Then there was a loud crash, like a door breaking. Several gunshots went off, and loud screams could be heard.

"I am sorry for everything," the commanding officer continued. "Oh god, they are here. Wait, no! Don't get away from me. Don't—"

The loud speaker went off, and nothing else could be heard.

"Well, let's get as much ammo and guns as we can carry," Master Chief said. "Hopefully we can find some more survivors."

"Do you think it's a good idea we leave here?" Barich asked. "I mean we don't know what they are, and we don't know how to kill them."

"If we wait here, we are going to get trapped and cause a lot of unnecessary attention, and I have an idea how to kill these bastards! Shoot 'em in the head!" Master Chief said.

. . . . .

Boats gathered everyone together and told them the plan. He was not the highest ranking person in the group, but he was the only one with a plan, so everyone listened, including Smith. Timmy would go out the port side door and create as much noise as possible. In the meantime, while the horde headed toward him, Boats and Danny and Smith would sneak out the other entrance.

Timmy was ready as Boats stood on the other side, ready for the signal. Slowly Timmy grabbed the handles and lifted each one individually. There were three in total. Getting to the second one, Timmy knew there was one more left. Grabbing it, a familiar voice was screaming on the other side, banging has hard as she could.

"Help me!" Cindy shouted. "Please let me in!"

"Oh my god!" Timmy exclaimed. "I'm coming! Wait!"

"NO, DON'T OPEN THAT GODDAMN DOOR!" Boats shouted. He took a metal dustpan and hit Timmy right in the back!

"Ouch! What the hell was that for?" Timmy said.

"She could be infected," Boats explained. "If she is, she will bring them right in here to us."

"No, I am not letting her die out there with them things," Timmy said.

Boats ran up to him and punched him in the face. Timmy fell back and got up, fists ready for him. Four others stepped in to break it up.

"Get *the fuck off* me!" Boats said. "Let me talk to her! *Let* me find out if she had contact with them. Cindy, you there?"

"Yes, Boats, I am here," Cindy replied.

"Are you injured, cut, any bite marks?"

Cindy was quiet and just cried. "Please let me in,"she said after a few moments.

"You know I cannot do that," Boats said.

"I know. I am sorry, Timmy."

"No, wait. So what does this mean?" Timmy said. "Are you going to be okay? No, please, God, open this fucking door!" Timmy ran to the door as other survivors held the door shut, preventing Timmy from letting her in. He knew he could not open it. She was infected. "I fucking hate you, Boats! You are a bastard!" he screamed at Boats, flicking him the finger. Her quiet sniffles could be heard as she accepted the inevitable.

"Don't get mad at him," Cindy said. "I am so scared."

"You know I care for you," said Timmy. "I wanted to be with you. This was not supposed to happen."

"It's okay. Promise me you will not forget me."

"I promise. Wait, you're going to be okay. We will get help. Just hold on."

"You know I regret a lot of things in my life. I hope you don't think that of me. I . . . I . . . I . . ."

Timmy, lying next to the door, heard her on the other side gasping for air. He could hear her breathing change, the fight of blood suffocating her breath. Her eyes turned white, her veins a dark purple, and the once-beautiful hair now was falling out. The pain was unbearable as she was ripping out her hair. Tiny grunts soon increased as she raged. Soon blood spewed from her mouth. Flailing her arms like a madman, she screamed as if her head was on fire. She then scratched on the door. She wanted to kill Timmy. Her only thought was to kill him and eat his flesh. He could hear her get angrier and more pissed off as the minutes grew.

Silence ensued on the survivors as they heard nothing but Cindy's screams and loud bangs on the door. Timmy cried to himself. Boats put his hand on Timmy, assuring him he would be okay. Timmy stood up and grabbed Boats by the neck. "Promise me something," He said.

"What is it, Timmy?" Boats asked.

If we don't make it through this"—tears rolled down his face—"if I know or you know we won't survive, end me before I change."

"Don't talk like that—"

"Fucking promise me you will kill me before they get to me!"

"I promise," Boats said. "You have my word."

# Chapter 6

## *The New Plan*

Jenny stood watch, often peeking up from behind the metal ladders outside by the catwalks. So far the walkers just kept to themselves, but there was so many of them. "So what are we going to do now?" Caleigh asked.

"Well, we were ordered not to leave the ship," Jenny replied. "As you can see, Big Navy is watching us."

"So are we just going to die here?" David said.

"There is another way," said Jenny. If we can make it to the island about five decks up where the bridge is, there is a radio. We can call the other ships and tell them we are alive, but getting there is going to be difficult. Creepers are everywhere.

"Shit," Caleigh cursed. "What about your helicopter? Is there a radio in—"

Jenny cut here off. "Are you serious? The minute they hear the radio, they will be all over us."

"Well, maybe there are other survivors," David put in. "I think if we wait here, we can—

Caleigh interrupted. "We can what? Huh, what can we do? We are running out of options."

David peeked, his eyes even with the deck of the flight deck, then something caught his eye, something disturbing. One of the undead was crawling up the walls of the island. This one looked different than the rest. It then stopped and smelled the air. Its back legs were inverted for climbing and leaping. Once a human, now it walked on all fours. Its tongue stretched longer as it stayed out of its mouth. "What the fuck is that?" David said to himself out loud. It then scurried to the other side out of view.

"What did you see?" Jenny asked.

"You don't want to know," he replied. "I have a feeling that if we don't think of something soon, we may not live to see the sun tomorrow."

. . . . .

Master Chief double-checked his weapons. He loaded up a green carry bag with enough ammo and rounds for all the weapons. To leave the area was all he wanted to do.

"Okay so, we are bringing three shotguns, eight of the 9MM pistols, and three M16s," Winston announced. "What about the M240?"

"I will carry it since you all have the guns and ammo," Andrew replied.

"No," Master Chief said. "Take the M16 and the pistol. I can haul that on my back. I think I can carry it. Besides, all I do is weight-lift. We can only bring one. Wish we had more help."

"So what is the plan?" Winston asked.

"We will go out the other way," Master Chief replied. "There are two ways down here, so while they are all on the port side, we will sneak out the starboard side. Once we are spotted, we will have to make a run for it. We will head for the life rafts. And it doesn't matter whichever one is closest. There are 127 out the catwalks, surrounding the flight deck of the carrier.

"*What?*" Andrew reacted. "Then why are we carrying all these weapons? What's the point, Master Chief? I thought the skipper said no one leaves."

"How many are onboard the ship? About six thousand, right? So what do you think will happen if we run out of ammo?" Master Chief said.

Silence grew as it finally sunk in. These guns were not for pleasure, but for last-minute if all else fails.

"We're fucked, huh, Master Chief?" Andrew said.

"Unless you want to get out of this, we need to work as a team," Master Chief said. "Now open that scuttle and peek up there, Winston."

. . . . .

Boats counted his makeshift weapons, double-checking everything. There can be no room for error. Checking his watch, he pondered a problem.

"What's wrong, Boats?" Smith asked.

"We need more bodies to go with us," Boats replied.

"Are you serious?" said Timmy. "What we are about to do is suicide. And besides, all the zombies are now banging at the door Cindy is at."

"I know," Boats said. "I think in a way she helped us. It's going to take four personal to lower the RHIB into the water. We got me—Timmy, since you don't have to distract them, you're coming—Danny, Smith, and we will need one other."

"Well, ask them," Timmy said. "That leaves sixteen personnel in here."

"Excuse me, everyone, I need a volunteer," Boats said. "We are attempting to leave the forecastle and get to one of the RHIB and lower it in the water. We are shorthanded a person. Is there anyone who is willing to help us? Anyone? I know this is a dangerous situation, but I need someone to . . ."

No one said a word as Boats looked upon everyone. Several of them outranked him but refused to say anything. In the back, he could see a young male officer staring at his marriage ring. Another senior chief kept his head down, not wanting to get involved. Then after a few minutes of silence, a small voice spoke, "I will go with you, Boats."

She stood only five foot five, and she was not even nineteen years of age. Her fingers adjusted her glasses as her short neck-length hair was pushed away from her face. She was in the back row. Some sailors had to move out of the way just so Boats could see her.

"What? No you just got here, Justine," Boats said.

"Does that matter anymore?" Justine replied. "I am small, and besides, if you are going to not pick me just because I am a girl, well—"

"Okay," Boats said before she could finish, "that is not what I was saying at all, but understand. You may not make it, I mean, you may . . ."

"Look, Justine said. "All my life I was told you can't do this. You can't do that. You're a girl. You're too small. Well, are you going to start that as well?"

"No," Timmy said. "Arm up, Justine. It just goes to show that you are braver than half of them."

The other shipmates hung their heads in shame. All were afraid of what was on the other side of that door.

"Before we go, can I say a prayer?" Smith said.

Boats nodded yes. If this was what was going to make him more alert, then Boats would entertain his words.

Everyone got down on one knee, and it reminded Boats of his high school days when he played football, and before the game, the priest would bless the team. His mind thought about in a few minutes all this would be on his shoulders, looking over the officers and chiefs in the room that refused to say a word or intervene. Boats noticed that Justine was not with them praying. He saw her writing something on a piece of paper. Tears hit the paper as she tried to wipe them, checking if anyone noticed her upset. Boats looked away before she noticed him looking at her, giving her time and peace with her thoughts.

Boats pondered to himself how they could call themselves leaders when in the time of crisis, they were nowhere to stepping up. His thoughts was interrupted with Smith saying, "Amen!" Everyone made the sign of the cross on their chest. "Game time," Boats said as he gave everyone a makeshift weapon.

"Lord Jesus, protects us," Smith said.

"Are you going to be doing this the whole time?" Boats asked him.

"Yes. Lord Jesus, protect us. Lord Jesus, protect us. Lord—"

"Silence!" Boats ordered. "Once we open that door, you need to seriously shut the hell up. I think he heard you the first hundred times. The noise will attract them."

Smith mouthed "whatever," mocking Boats.

Boats grabbed Smith's right arm and swung him around getting right in his face. "Hey, Smith, I hope you are at peace with God because if you do not kill them, they will not think twice killing you. When they come for us, if you become one of them, I will not hesitate one second to stop you."

Smith nodded yes as his hands holding the spear shook. Boats stopped and patted him on the back. Maybe he was being too hard on him, he thought.

Timmy started opening the door handles on the starboard side slowly. Cracking the door open, he saw that it was all clear from his vantage point. He signaled with his finger to move. Like a SWAT team member, Timmy checked the passageway. To the left was the berthing where sailors slept, its door already opened. There was an undead feeding on leftover limbs. He was not concerned of the living survivors coming out of the forecastle area. His teeth was rotten from eating as blood seeped from his hands, and he crunched on the bones of the fingers. Timmy walked back slowly and told everyone there was one outside all alone, feeding. He suggested they try to approach it and, if it was hostile, try to kill it, find out the best way to take them down. Everyone agreed.

Timmy went first, standing only ten feet away this thing that was gorging on human fingers, sucking the blood and all the meat out. It stopped and turned around, looking directly at Timmy. His face was not human anymore, hissing at Timmy, its hands extended as it ran toward him. Timmy warned him to stop, and with a quick thrust of the spear—its end a tied jagged knife—Timmy stabbed him in the stomach. He limped over and stayed quiet.

"See? That was easy, huh? Timmy turned toward Boats.

The creature hissed and went crazy, swinging and trying to reach Timmy. With a quick thrust, Boats ran and beheaded him. The infected fell and lived no more.

"Well, now we know how to stop them," Boats said. "We separate their heads or damage their brains."

Blood and drag marks were everywhere. The berthing door halfway ripped off the hinges was evidence that this was not a good place to hide. With Timmy watching the door, Boats, Justine, Danny, and Smith ran past, checking the next area. It was like a SWAT team, the way they moved, being as quiet as possible and only using hand signals. Cutting to the right was a ladder well heading to the tunnel. This was where the AIMD department worked out of. All parts for planes were ordered from this spot. This was also the entrance to the hangar bays. Boats stepped slowly as he could see a little more the lower he got down the ladder. "Shit," he whispered. There were three of them just wondering in their way. They stood there, moving very little. Boats gestured with three fingers and pointed down. He then pointed at his eyes. He then pointed at himself, the next in line, and the one behind that guy to follow him. Everyone else stayed put.

Slowly Boats, Timmy, and Danny crept behind them. Using his knife, Boats slit his victim's neck, sawing his throat, so as not to alert the other creepers. Danny stabbed his foe in the right eye and twisted. It made a smooch sound. And Timmy took a sledgehammer to the right temple of the dead. Quietly Boats snapped his fingers rapidly, and Smith and Justine soon followed. Cracking the next door, they could see the hangar bay. Hundreds of them were all blocking the way to the RHIB. "Dammit, there is no way we are going to make it," Boats said.

Timmy took a peek and shook his head. "Impossible, guys, we would have to run seventy-five feet, cut to the right, run about twenty-five feet, and run along the walls. That's about three hundred feet before we reach the entrance to the RHIBs to the right."

Boats stood there mad at himself. He had no choice but head back up to the forecastle, and this was utter madness to attempt with primitive weapons.

"What are we going to do?" Smith asked.

"Nothing," Boats answered him. "Unless we have some kind of distraction, we can't make it. There are too many of them."

Justine thought for a moment and pulled out a piece of folded paper. Kissing it, she left lipstick marks on it, and she slid it into Timmy's pocket. "Hey, do me a favor, guys. Make sure that if you make it, take that letter to my husband whom I—Well, he already knows how much I love him."

Boats overheard the conversation, but his reaction was too late. All he saw were tears from her eyes as she ran past him pushing through the double doors, heading right for them all in a full sprint. Once she reached the hangar bay, she screamed and cut to the left. The horde was awake and followed in hot pursuit behind her. Boats could see hundreds of them all active now, running for her. From his view, they ran from right to the left side after her. She created a small window for them.

Justine ran as fast as she could, ducking their swings, dodging their teeth from those she ran past, collecting more of them. The loud howls of the dead craved her young flesh. Some were crawlers. She jumped over them when they swung for her legs. One turned around slowly. Justine faked right and kneed him in the stomach, quickly pushing him face first on the deck. She did this often, creating an obstacle for the thirsty blood-hunting horde.

Boats saw no more running coming from the right side. It must have been clear as he screamed, "RUN NOW! GO AS FAST AS YOU! CAN GET TO THE RHIB! NO MATTER WHAT HAPPENS, DON'T STOP! Damn, that girl is fucking crazy."

"She could have at least grabbed a weapon!" Timmy said. "Fuck, look at them. They are all going after her!"

. . . . .

Opening up the small hatch, Winston slowly stuck his M16 gun up the entrance. All of a sudden, something grabbed it, trying to yank it out of his grip. The struggle ceased as he opened fire and heard the dead let go. It cried and fell to the floor. "Holy shit, that was close! We aren't even through the hatch yet," he said excitedly. Sticking his head through, he could see that the creature lay motionless on the ground. The angle of which the gun was fired put blood spots on the ceiling, dripping to the floor and making spattering sounds. Nothing else was around. Andrew soon followed. Knowing that Master Chief was not going to fit the M240 through, they decided to open the entire hatch.

"Okay, everyone, take your safety off your guns," Master Chief ordered. "If you see any of them with TLD badges on their belts, kill them on spot. Headshots! Make them count!"

Andrew and Winston had this puzzled look on their face, wanting to know why.

Master Chief said, "They are the smart ones. Trust me."

He pointed to a sign that said "Hangar Bay," with an arrow pointing up the ladder well. Below it was another sign saying "Flight Deck" pointing up as well. Andrew pointed and got the okay nod from Master Chief to proceed with caution. Walking up the ladder well, they heard a large horde screaming from the door leading into the hangar bay. Winston took a peek and saw hundreds of them running after something. Master Chief went to take a look as Andrew kept watch on both ladder wells heading up and down just in case they got flanked. From his view, Master Chief saw a small girl running for her life. She was sweating and gasping for air as the hundreds were only five feet behind her. *What a brave girl she must be, but why is she running in the open? Why isn't she hiding?* he thought.

Justine remembered her track days when she ran cross-country—to keep a strong pace, not to let up the long distance. Her plan was to keep them busy as long as Boats and the others got to the RHIB. She figured they would need time to lower the boat about sixty to seventy feet into the water. This would take a few minutes. Her shins were starting to hurt as she wished she had running shoes. Then again running on the hard nonskid was serving as no cushion to her feet. In the back of Hangar BIII were storage boxes on either side with a narrow passage, and she decided to cut into it. As she increased distance, she realized what a fatal mistake she made. Hundreds of them were hot on her trail, and some fifty of them cut to the left. Another seventy cut to the right, trying to flank her. The majority followed her. She cut to the left and saw them in front of her. Cutting to the right behind the storage boxes, she saw others in front of her, trapping her escape. Quickly she climbed on the boxes, getting as high as she can. Since she was so small, it was easy for her. The clumsy creatures were not as graceful. Getting to the top, she could see everything.

Catching her breath, she realized that there was nowhere else to run, and these things were staring to climb to her all round her. A few of them climbed fast. Reaching the last box, Justine lay on her knees with her hands covering her head, soaked in sweat. It was the end. The walker, now a climber, reached for her and went teeth out for the back of her neck.

A loud gunshot went off three times fast. She looked up and saw the creature inches from her, and with his hand out, it stopped. Another three automatic gunshots went ripping near her. This time, the creature fell back down the boxes. Another was behind her as she heard the bullet whip near her right ear, hitting the zombie in the face. Master Chief was picking them off one by one with the M16. Four more attempted to kill her, but the marksmanship of Master Chief was impressive. Then they all charged Master Chief, and he switched to automatic. He opened their heads with led. The empty shells hit the deck, and blood flew everywhere. The horde was thinning out due to the trigger finger of master chief. Justine could see that she was not the only survivor, and she waved with excitement, as Master chief picked off the last remaining few that were still approaching. Eventually there were no zombies left standing. She climbed down, running toward Master Chief who cleared the path with bloody destruction.

Walking toward Master Chief, Justine smiled, saying, "Oh, thank God you came. I didn't know how much more I could run."

Master Chief, his hearing temporarily damaged by the automatic fire shouted at Justine as he reloaded, "ARE YOU FUCKING CRAZY? WHAT THE HELL! DO YOU SERIOUSLY HAVE A DEATH WISH?"

Justine waited a few moments and said, "No, wait. You don't understand. I was trying—"

As she was about to explain that there were other survivors and she was only trying to distract the infected, one of the creatures jumped on her. It must have been a fifteen-foot leap. It landed right on top of her, and it had enormous strength, dragging Justine's right arm. It happened so fast, she had no time to react. It dragged her on the sharp nonskid, and her back and back legs bled from the rough surface. This thing was fast. She screamed in pain. As if the dragging wasn't enough, it pulled her so hard around the corners. It had no regard for her, ripping her arm and dislocating it from the joint. The triple pop of her bone from her joints made her shriek out a horrible scream. Her leg was caught around one of the turns, and the creature pulled and pulled with two hands, and finally it twisted her arm three times to the left then four times to the right until it was severed. The pain was unbearable.

By the time Master Chief reloaded his gun, Justine was gone, abducted. He ran toward the scream, Winston right behind him as well.

Heading toward her cries, they rounded the corners and saw her lying there. She was alone. No creature was near her. Master Chief called out to her, but he received no answer. All he saw was her other hand moving slightly. He walked towards her, but something made Master Chief stop dead in his tracks. Looking up, he saw it.

"Why the hell are we stopping?" Winston asked.

"Look up there. It's one of the smart ones. These fuckers set a trap," Master Chief answered.

"I don't think so," Winston said. It's dead. It cannot problem-solve. Here, take my gun. I will get her."

"No, we leave now," said Master Chief. "She is the bait, and they are trying to lure us to her."

"Fuck this! I can get her," Winston insisted. He ran to Justine and picked up her head. She was lying on her stomach on the rough surface. She was cut pretty bad. She moaned in the uncomfortable position she lay.

"HEY YOU!" Master Chief hollered. "YEAH, FUCKER, OVER HERE! GET ME, COME ON! COME FOR ME! YOU KNOW YOU WANT ME!

As he fired some rounds in the air, the creature waited for the trap, and a loud monsterlike howl came from him. The horde ran in an almost sprintlike fashion. Toward the dinner bell. Master Chief got the hell out of there. Even if he could kill some of them, by the time he reloaded, he would get swarmed. He retreated to Andrew who was peeking in the entrance way. Andrew flung his arms in the air saying, "What the fuck? Where is Winston and that chick?"

Master Chief didn't say anything, and Andrew already knew the answer.

Winston tried to help her up. When he turned around, he realized he was surrounded. Grabbing for his pistol, he realized that he gave his gun to Master Chief. *How stupid can you be?* he thought to himself.

The smart one jumped down from the top ledge. Its skin was gone, nothing but flesh and exposed muscles. Justine rolled on her back, "What the hell are you waiting for? Finish it already."

The creature howled, and the horde all backed away as if something was about to happen. She could feel the vibration of something big coming closer, shaking the ground with the constant pounding of heavy footsteps until it revealed itself.

A monster stood eight feet tall. With its huge teeth and massive muscles, this thing was a giant. Grabbing Justine by the back of her hair, it held her by her scalp. Its breath was of puke and death. Her feet dangled four feet off the ground. With a loud roar, it opened its mouth big enough to fit her head in it, and with the compression of its massive jaw, it crushed her skull, brains oozing out the sides of his mouth. Blood flowed everywhere as this monster chewed on. While it crunched on the broken skull pieces, he held the the neck and rest of Justine's body limp in its massive hand. He took it and threw it to the wall about fifteen feet where the blood smeared down the wall. The, horde in a frenzy, ran toward the lifeless body lying on the ground. It now turned its attention at Winston.

Master Chief quietly shut the door and heared Winston screaming in agony and bloody pain from that freak of nature. There was nothing he could do.

"I told him not to get her!" Master Chief said. "Dammit, Andrew, why didn't he listen?"

"I don't know," Andrew relpied. "What do we do now?"

"We head to the flight deck. We stick to the plan."

# Chapter 7

## *ACTS OF AGGRESSION*

Timmy jumped in the RHIB, taking off the belly straps. Smith was directed to unclip the bottom ones.

"Good, now the aft one," Timmy said. "You're doing good, Smith."

Danny was on the top deck, quickly slacking the forward and aft steady lines. Boats jumped into the RHIB, saying, "We are seriously shorthanded. Since we're dead in the water, I'm taking off the steady lines. Danny, you control the winch and swing up then out."

Danny turned on the winch controls, coming up about twelve inches. The RHIB was now free of the cradle. Boats did the signaled for Danny to swing it out. While Danny was swinging out, the long monkey lines were dropped from the RHIB to the water's surface. These were safety lines attached to the overhead so personnel could holds on to them in case the cable snaps.

"Wait," Smith said. "Do you hear that? Sounds like gunshots coming from the hangar bay. I think were safe."

"I hope Justine escaped," Boats said. "Danny, lower the RHIB. Keep one monkey line up there. When I am in the water, climb down the one I left up there for you. Make sure you grab Smith."

Timmy, already inside the boat, turned on the CB radio, trying different channels and hoping frantically for a response. "This is a United State Air Craft Carrier. We are alive. We are not infected! *Anyone*, we have survivors. We are attempting to leave the warship. Hello, this is Seaman Timmy. We are not infected. I repeat, we are not infected."

The RHIB was lowered into the water about forty feet below. Boats held on while Timmy continued to call out. Five feet from the water, he cranked the engine. The *putt putt* soon roared as the engine turned over, and the propellers circulated in the water. Smith, guarding the entrance into the RHIB deck, watched the ladder wells and made sure there were no surprises. Once the RHIB hit the water, the hook was released, and all lines were released.

The radio crackled, and a voice said, "Hello, this is Warship 64. We understand your situation. You are not authorized to leave the vessel. Do you understand? We will execute deadly force if you do not get back on the ship."

"Listen to me," Boats said. "I am Boatswain's Mate—*shit*, the ship is overrun. We are not infected. Do you understand? We have survivors!"

"This is Warship 67," came another voice on the radio. "I confirm with Warship 64 that you are not authorized to leave the vessel. Anyone leaving the area will be considered a threat to national security and will be terminated on spot."

"Are they serious?" Timmy said. "We are not the bad guys here! This is bullshit!"

Smith stood guard as Danny gave him the thumbs-up that the RHIB was in the water. In that moment, an infected one crept up the ladder well. Smith called out, "Justine, is that you?" Smith froze with terror as it approached him.

Danny could see Smith backing away from the door, allowing the dead to walk in. Smith held on to the mop handle spear, shaking and backing up. His face, his expression was as if he was literally scared of death. The infected hobbled into the RHIB area, stiff arms extending as the shiny cross on the collar revealed why Smith was so scared. If it was any other infected, Smith would have not thought twice, but this one was the chaplain.

"WHAT ARE YOU DOING SMITH?" Danny shouted. "KILL HIM!"

"I . . . I . . ." Smith stammered, "Can't . . . I can't!"

The creature ran toward Smith whose reaction was not to do anything, but instincts overpowered his motive as he held the spear in front of the creature. Stabbing him through the left side of his chest, Smith could feel it go through its chest bone, through his heart, and exit the other end of his back. The combination of crunching and ripped flesh almost made Smith sick to his stomach. It slumped over, not moving as Smith cried, "I am so sorry. Oh, God, please forgive me. I am so sorry." It lay motionless with the spear in its chest and Smith holding the other end, so scared to even let go. All Smith could do was stare at the cross emblem. Crying, he begged and begged for forgiveness for this immoral act that he executed.

Danny watched in utter horror as a few more entered the space. Smith saw them as well, and his eyes were focused on them now. The creature, still connected to the spear, grunted as blood spit out of its mouth. Picking up his head, his eyes were cold, bloody nothings. His arms and hands rose, slowly grabbing the spear with two hands. The creature then pushed it in farther, and this reaction caused Smith to get closer to him. Grunting louder, it pulled harder as the spear passed through its decaying body. Now Smith was just inches away from him, still holding on to the wooden spear. Danny screamed, "SMITH, LET GO! GET THE FUCK OUT OF THERE! JUMP OVER THE SIDE!"

Danny jumped down one deck since the stairs were invaded by the dead. He then spit on both hands and leaped for the monkey lines. Swinging, he looked below to see if the RHIB was still there. It was about fifteen yards out. Climbing down as fast as he could, he could no longer see the deck above where Smith was. He heard a scuffle and assumed the worse. About ten feet from the water, he let go and splashed into the water. Boats swung the engine around to pick him up. As Danny was brought into the RHIB, a loud scream could be heard from above, and the black silhouette of a person jumping made everyone look up. None of the dead dare to follow. There was a loud splash, and Smith surfaced moments after swinging his arms.

"Fuck, he can't swim," Timmy said.

"I got him," Boats said. "Keep up with the radio. We need to head to the bow area, and hopefully, the line is in place so we can get the others out of here.

Smith grabbed on to Danny for dear life, coughing saltwater and trying to catch his breath. He kept thanking everyone over and over as he was brought into the RHIB.

"Hey, it's okay," Danny said. "Did you get bitten? Scratched?"

"No, I am okay," Smith replied. Holding his right shoulder, he felt a sharp sting, and he lay on it so the others could not see.

He was bitten.

. . . . .

Master Chief climbed up the metal stairs. Playing over and over in his head was that young girl and the stupidity of Winston. *Who was she, and what the hell was she doing?*

"We're on the 03 deck." Andrew said. "The life rafts should be outside one of these doors."

Opening up the door, he discovered three zombies lying stiff and slumped on the door. Master Chief shot them at point-blank range. Blood spewed all over, and he wiped his face, making sure none got in his mouth. Located on the catwalk, they realized they came up the wrong entrance leading to the life raft. There was none near them. A bunch was a hundred feet forward, but in order to get to them, they would have to gun along the flight deck.

Looking at the calm sea, both Master Chief and Andrew saw a lot of U.S. warships about five miles out, surrounding the crippled carrier.

Shaking his head from the short distraction, Master Chief devised a new plan. "I will distract them," he said. "Do you know how to release the life rafts?"

"Yes, Master Chief, "Adrew replied. Before I was a quartermaster, I used to be on deck, and they showed me how to release them."

"Make it quick"

Without a second thought, Master Chief walked onto the flight deck. The undead noticed his presence and walked and bumped into one another. Clicking the M16's safety off, Master Chief opened fire with three-round bursts so as to save ammo. He made clean shots to the head, and they fell one by one. The sound and echo from the discharge made them active once again as they started running, picking up speed toward Master Chief.

Andrew Barich ran behind him, along the side, and jumped down to the catwalk to the first life raft. He released the sea painter, but it did not leave it carriage holder. Andrew used his foot to push it over the side. He kicked it repeatedly until it released and fell into the water. The loud splash assured him it was in the ocean. However, looking over the side, he discovered that it did not activate. "SHIT! HEY, MASTER CHIEF, IT WAS A DUD! GOING TO RELEASE ANOTHER ONE!" he screamed. Same as before, it had to be pushed. This time, it fell and activated. The gray shell casing cracked like an egg as a yellow life raft inflated in the water.

Master Chief continued to lay pumped led into the infected, dropping one by one. They still advanced onward to the living. Those who fell or who were not shot completely crawled as well.

Andrew screamed for Master Chief, but his M16 was switched to automatic and he could not hear him. Five of them made their way on the catwalk, running at Andrew. He drew his pistol from his side and aimed for their heads. There were two left, but something was different. These were dodging his bullets! How could something move so fast. Dropping his clip, he grabbed another. But he had no time to click it into the gun. They were right on top of him. He ducked low and flipped them both over the side as they lunged for him. "Royal Rumble, bitch! WHAT" he said as they fell below. Waiting for the splash, he realized what a bad mistake that was as they landed on the yellow life raft. A loud roar could be heard overhead as two FA18 fighters approached. Smiling, Andrew waved.

Then everything changed. The locked target was not the zombies. It was the life raft as a missile ejected a path of white smoke behind it and turned for the raft. A huge explosion disintegrated the life raft into a mushroom cloud. "No, this can't be!" he said as he ran to release another life raft. Master Chief continued to open fire with the M16. Looking to the direction of the explosion, he shouted "WHAT THE HELL WAS THAT?"

The FA-18 flew by and circled hard to the left, making a maneuverable turn. Its jet engines could be heard as it turned, heading away. Andrew quickly released another. As it splashed into the water, they heard the faint sound of the FA18 once again as it turned back toward the ship. The thrusters increased louder as it now released another missile at the deployed life raft. Another explosion sent it up in pieces.

"Shit, I don't fucking believe this!" Andrew said. "They are blowing up our only way out of here. THIS IS BULLSHIT!"

"Shit, we need another plan," said Master Chief.

Frustrated, he could see from a distance three people running toward the island. It looked like two civilians and a female officer. Some of the runners saw the movement and changed direction from Master Chief to their new target.

"Hey wheels Andrew Barich," Master Chief said. "Get your ass up here. I need your help! We got more survivors!"

. . . . . "5 minutes prior" . . . . .

Caleigh, Jenny and David waited, keeping quiet. Thinking how great it would be to have a shower right now, Caleigh grinned. The constant running and sleeping in the same clothes made her very self-conscious of body odor. David got up and peeked over toward the island part of the carrier, often checking if the dead have moved so they could make a run for it. He shook his head, and it was apparent Jenny and Caleigh both know the answer.

"We have to do something," Jenny said. "We just can't sit here waiting until we get discovered by them—wait, do you hear that?"

"What is that noise?" Caleigh asked.

"Sounds like a boat," David said. "Oh shit, we're saved!"

Caleigh and Jenny jumped up, leaning over the rail of the catwalk and looking below. Nothing. They could not see it. But they could hear it. Then there was a splash as if someone jumped in the water.

Caleigh took off her shoes and quickly tied her hair back, trying to climb over the rails.

"Wait," Jenny said. "Don't even think about it. The fall would kill you if you hit the water the wrong way. It's more like hitting concrete."

"Hell no! Are you crazy?" David said. "Think about what you're doing. We're about eighty to a hundred feet above the water."

Caleigh slowly came back over, listening to reason and leaning over to see the boat that was hidden from view.

"Shit. get down!" Jenny said suddenly.

Just then, a walker saw Jenny duck her blonde hair from view. It staggered toward them. If it got right by the ladder heading toward the catwalk, they will be discovered. Moaning, two more walkers looked in their direction and soon followed. David waited with his belt, knowing that if it saw them, this would be a fight for their lives. They stayed close under the ladder while blood dripped on the steps. The oozing soon dripped from the walker, hitting cross metal grill steps and on to the survivor's clothes.

Caleigh closed her eyes as tears ran down her face while Jenny held her hand over her mouth and was on the verge of hyperventilating. The infected rslammed his right foot down, stepping on the first step and going down another. A few seconds later, it moved to its other foot, which had a partially torn uniform revealing exposed flesh around its calf muscle. Only inches underneath, David could hear the other ones not that far behind. Hitting the third step down, David understood what he would have to do. Gripping his belt as tight as possible around his hands, he waited for the corpse to make one more step for the ambush. The other zombies were soon to follow.

It stopped as the echoes of gun firing could be heard on the other side of the flight deck. Turning around, it retreated and headed toward the new attraction. Both Caleigh and Jenny blew out a huge sigh of relief as it disappeared back on the flight deck. David ran to see what was going on. In the distance, a man stood a little over six feet tall, his huge arm muscles flexed as he held the M16. "Damn, I feel sorry for them bastards," he smiled rooting for the man with weapons.

It was Master Chief, alone standing and popping them one by one. Every bullet hitting them made blood splatter as more were attracted to the repeated cracking of each gunshot leaving the M16. The constant ping of gun shells hitting the flight deck was proof that this was one fucker who was not to be messed with.

David looked at the island as more of the undead were drawn to the excitement. They came from everywhere. Falling from the bridge, some broke their legs, but they still advanced onward toward the sounds. The horde was becoming frenzied, each wanting to kill Master Chief.

Jenny peeked out as she heard a familiar sound. Scanning the skies, Caleigh pointed up as fighter jets roared overhead, waving both arms at them. One turned around as it approached the port side of the ship. Caleigh David and Jenny were located on the opposite starboard side of the area. A loud explosion could be heard. Caleigh screamed, "What the hell was that?"

David had no idea as Jenny didn't understand what was going on the other side of the ship.

There was another flyby as one of the jets came around, followed by another explosion. David questioned, "Wait. Are they firing at us?"

Jenny could not explain what they were doing, but she could clearly see the trail of smoke from the missile. She then said, "No one is near the island. Let's make a run for it. GO! GO! Don't stop!"

Running without regard for anything, the three of them headed toward the island. Jenny, the fastest out of the group, ran toward the door leading up to the island. Caleigh was about fifteen feet behind and David about twenty-five feet behind her. Gasping for breath, David stopped for a second. About ten of the dead saw him. He was much closer than Master Chief. Shifting direction, they headed right for him.

Caleigh reached the door and looked back as new zombies now blocked David's path, separating them.

David soon was getting surrounded as they closed the gap. These creatures wanted fresh meat. Snapping and yelling at each other, the zombies soon realized food was scarce. As one lunged for David, a single bullet whizzed at the dead, and it walked no more, lying motionless at David's feet. The torn uniform was the only evidence that this was once human. Another fell, soon another. One by one they went down.

Master Chief and Andrew ran toward David with reinforcement weapons. Andrew, knowing he was still a great distance, opted to even the odds. Leaning back as far as he could, he threw a 9MM pistol up in the air toward David screaming, "Hey, heads up!"

David saw it coming back down to earth as it spun. Cupping both his hands, he caught it, slowing down its fall. A walker swung, and David fell on his back, aiming at his devourer. He fired. The bullet ripped through below its chin and into its head. David rolled to his right as another tried to step on his face. Grabbing his leg, David pushed it forward, unbalancing it. As it fell, David stood up holding his leg and shot him in the face. Three more grabbed for his back but were at the hands of Andrew and Master Chief putting them down. Now back to back. all three of them were surrounded.

"Hey, long time no see," David said. "Thanks for the help."

"Sure," said Andrew. "Now how the hell are we going to get out of this one?"

"I GOT THIS!" Master Chief bellowed. "EVERYONE, DUCK AND COVER YOUR EARS!"

Reaching behind, he swung the M240. The long barrel was going to unleash massive destruction for anything staring at its end. He cocked the ammo into the chamber add released the handle. The spring clicked the first bullet ready. Holding on the barrel with one hand, he squeezed the trigger. *THUNG THUNG THUNG THUNG THUNG THUNG THUNG THUNG*! This massive gun unleashed devastation on anything that stood in its path. Ripping right through their flesh, the gun created massive entry and exit wounds. The sound was so loud and deafening that both David and Andrew held their palms over their ears as tight as they could as Master Chief created an exit. Heads were completely severed, limbs were cut off, and flesh exploded as the bullets impacted on the bodies of the infected. The visions of flashes of lights gave it the illusion that the M240 was shooting lasers, but it was the massive heat of the bullets exiting the barrel.

Master Chief tapped Andrew and David on the shoulder as the stayed low, hiding their faces from the shell casings often flying out the other end and hitting them in the back. David looked up. Nothing was standing. Blood was everywhere. Shell casings, hundreds of them, lay around Master Chief's polished military boots.

A loud scream could be heard for about fifteen seconds as all three looked in the aft direction. The lone monster calling for reinforcements was soon heading in their direction. More infected made their way up the flight deck. Andrew suggested, "I think we should fold our hand and get the hell out of dodge."

All agreed as they headed toward Jenny and Caleigh. They worked toward the door, closed it, and made their way up four decks to the navigational bridge. Walking in, a crawler reached for them but was stopped by the 9MM. Master Chief secured the door, putting a chain around it. He then walked toward the front windows that wrapped completely around the full view of the flight deck that was slowly filling up with infected. And in the distance, the presence of warships could be seen.

"Hey, Barich, get on the radio and call those ships," Master Chief said. "Find out why they blew up our—you know, never mind. Tell them we are alive. Hurry up! I don't know how much longer we can hold out here."

Looking out the window, Jenny saw her helicopter untouched and tied down on the flight deck. She breathed a sigh of relief as a thought planned in her head for the escape. Her step-by-step procedure was interrupted as she put her ear in the direction of the bow of the ship.

"What is it Jenny?" Caleigh asked." You see something?"

"I don't know," Jenny replied. I could have sworn I heard gunshots go off. I heard it. I know I did. It sounded like three or four of them."

"There may be others?" David said. "Alive."

"They may already be dead," Master Chief chimed in.

# Chapter 8

## *No Room for Errors*

Boats headed for the bow of the massive carrier. Looking up the hole entrances, he saw that no line was dropped. He honked the RHIB horn. On the starboard side, a line fell, hitting the water. Boats swung the boat around. Approaching the makeshift line, Danny grabbed on to it. He could see sailors waving and clapping, happy to see them.

"Hey, Boats, what are we going to do?" Timmy asked. "The other vessels are acting aggressive towards us still."

"Fuck it," Boats said. "Let's get them down from there. I'll deal with the repercussions later. Danny hold on to that—"

A shot was fired, and it hit the outboard engine of the RHIB. Boats ducked, looking in the direction of one of the warships where it possibly came from. Boats told everyone to keep low as he attempted to swing the engine around out of the shooter's view. Another gunshot echoed. This time it ricocheted, sparking as it hit the engine. "WHAT THE FUCK! STOP SHOOTING!" Boats screamed as if they could hear him. Two more gunshots hit the outboard engine, causing damage to it. The RHIB's single engine was now building white smoke. Boats tried to gun the engine forward, but it did not respond. He then reversed the throttle, and it moved. When he went forward on it again, it kept in reverse. He realized the RHIB was broken, going in a counterclockwise motion in reverse speed.

"They called us on the radio," Timmy said. "If we don't get back on the ship, the next time they will not miss."

"Well, we don't have a choice now," said Boats. "Timmy, go grab the line when we come around again and hold it."

When the boat came around the line that was connected to the forecastle holes, Timmy reached and stopped the boat. The other end must have been tied on top to something secure.

Danny went to the back of the boat to tell Smith what was going on. He was lying there on his injured shoulder. Danny pushed his other shoulder from its side to him on his back, "Hey, Smith, wake up! We got to get out of here, Smith. You okay? Hey, buddies, can you—"

Smith grabbed Danny by his shirt and bit him right in the chest. Danny had no time to react. His only option was punching him hard, and his repellings were enough to free him. Falling back, he put his hand on his chest and looked up at Boats. Feeling the wound, he kept looking at the blood on his fingers as it gushed out inside the RHIB.

"Boats, get the hell out of here!" Danny said. "He got me! Hurry! BEFORE I—"

"OH SHIT!" Boats shouted. "NO! OH GOD, FUCK! NO! TIMMY, CLIMB NOW!"

"Who is going to hold the line to the RHIB?" Timmy counterd. "YOU GO FIRST! I SWEAR I WILL BE RIGHT BEHIND YOU!"

Boats could see Danny choking on his own blood. His eyes were rolling in the back of his head. He was trying to fight the transformation. His veins were filling dark with the infection. Holding his head, he now felt the pain of what everyone else must have felt. Screaming, he was like a mad man!

Boats leaped on the line, climbing back up to the forecastle. Pulling with his forearms, locking his legs around the line, he pulled himself higher and higher. Adrenaline was kicking in as he raced back into the forecastle. Once he reached the entrance, one of the survivors grabbed him with one hand and pulled him off his feet back on the forecastle. He lay catching his breath while his arms ached. "TIMMY!" he screamed.

He could not see there were too many people blocking the small view to where the line led out to where Timmy was. He could hear everyone screaming at Timmy.

After Timmy saw Boats clear the forecastle, he tugged the line to make sure it would hold. He was a skinny kid, and this was a long hike. Nervous, he was not too fond of heights. The roar of the infected zombie trying to grab him was enough motivation to go. He climbed up the line, and the RHIB separated from it. Timmy swung but held on until the swinging ceased. Now fifteen feet from the water he could see the RHIB still going in circles in reverse. He could see infected Smith screaming and waving his arms inside the boat, "Where the hell is the—" He felt the line moving and looked down. Danny was also climbing. "OH SHIT! OH SHIT!" he screamed as he raced to the top. Danny, now infected, was much faster, his feet hanging as he pulled with his right hand then his left, constant blood spewing from his mouth. Timmy could not believe this super strength Danny possessed. It was obvious, and everyone was screaming to Timmy to hurry. Timmy, only ten feet to the entrance, screamed, "SOMEONE THROW ME A FUCKING KNIFE! HURRY!"

That's what they did. Timmy looked up and saw an open knife, blade first, headed right for him. He dodged out of the way as it whizzed right past him, hitting infected Danny in the right eye. With its falling velocity and speed, there was no way he was going to catch it. "Maybe in the movies but not while holding on a line," he said out loud. Looking down, he saw it embedded in Danny's eye. His cold decay look could not see what hit him. Danny screamed, more pissed off than before. Holding on with one hand, he reached for the handle and pulled the knife out his eye. His eyeball and socket followed as he ripped it, throwing it in the water.

Timmy was scared to death. Looking at the black void where Danny's eye once was, he raced as fast as he could to keep his life.

Getting to the top of the entrance, a shipmate grabbed the back of his collar, throwing him on the forecastle. This sailor then untied the end and let the line go.

As the end of the line left the forecastle, the infected Danny was racing up the line fast as a cat trying not to get wet. With lightning speed, he moved, but there was no more line to grab. With one desperate leap, it jumped for the forecastle opening.

There were too many people with their heads out the viewports, and they were not paying attention when the line ran freely. Danny, now infected, grabbed the one unsuspecting sailor around the neck. His name was Seaman Dorsey. He screamed as he was getting pulled out the forecastle into the water. With his nails dug deep in the victim's neck, Danny did a pull-up, gripping his throat and was biting chunks of flesh off his face. Spitting out the skin, he craved blood.

Frantically everyone was holding on to him and screaming, trying to pull him up. It was a tug of war. Boats lay on his back on the floor exhausted, looking at the sailor who pulled him up. He shook his head no. The sailor nodded and walked over to where the victim was getting mauled. Grabbing his legs, he told everyone to let go, assuring that he got him. The other survivors saw the strength this sailor had as he pulled two up with one hand. What took four guys to hold on, this meathead could do alone.

Once everyone let go, he flipped him over the side. Danny held on to his meal as they both fell to the water. Poor Seaman Dorsey was just in the wrong place at the wrong time. About ten feet before the water impact, two shots echoed, one hitting Danny and the other hitting its victim. A sniper shot hitting a midair target was excellent marksmanship.

"snipers" someone screamed.

"Hey, thanks for the help, Collado," Boats said.

"Sure," Collado said. "That was fucking intense. Timmy, you fucking must really want to live. That knife was supposed to hit you. I didn't want to pull up two infections."

**95**

"Thanks, asshole," Timmy said. "The only person who's gonna kill me is Boats."

Boats smiled as he patted Timmy on the back. He remembered.

Jose Collado was considered a "deck ape." His huge arms made it apparent that this guy was a weightlifter. Hispanic, he stood over six feet with a broad chest. Despite his appearance, he was what Boats called a soft bully. His work attitude kept him alive for this long. *Maybe he would be more useful than sweeping spaces,* Boats thought to himself.

Thinking on everything that just happened, Boats was exhausted. Looking around, he couldn't believe that he was back on the forecastle. Scanning, he realized there was more people up here than when he left. Off an estimate, there were probably about sixty personnel. "How did all these people get up here?" he asked. "Where did they all come from?"

"Everywhere," Jose replied. "Some were smart to avoid the high-traffic areas. Most got up here from some girl distracting the main entrance in the hangar bay. Thanks to her, we snuck past the horde and made it safe up here."

"Does anyone know what hap—"

"I don't think she survived, Boats."

Silence fell as Timmy felt bad about Justine. Then he remembered his back pocket, the letter she gave him. He pulled it out, and something hit the deck and made a *ping* sound. Looking next to his boot, he picked up her wedding ring that was left in the letter.

Boats walked over toward Timmy. "You sure you want to read it?"

Timmy wiped the sweat from his forehead and said to Boats, "What if we don't make it? I mean, look at what happened. We tried to escape and we was fired on. I don't know if we are doing the right thing. I lost Cindy. Look, I know what you are thinking, and I don't talk about my personal life, but yeah, everyone knows I had a fiancé, and I left her because I called her two in the morning and some guy answered her phone."

"Maybe it was—"

"No, it was her house phone. She keeps it by her bed. Come on, do you think I am that stupid?"

It was obvious Boats knew this was a touchy subject, and rather than add fuel to the fire, he changed the subject. "Hey, Timmy, did you get any water? Are you thirsty?"

"Excuse me, Excuse me, shipmates!" an officer announced his presence to Boats and Timmy.

Boats put his hands over his head and said under his breath, "Christ, not one of these pencil dicks." To the officer, he said, "Yes."

"Yes what?" the officer said. "It's 'yes, sir.'"

"Okay, sir, can I entertain you?"

"Don't lose your military bearing, shipmate. You are still addressing an officer."

"Sir," Jose cut in. "There is no need for—"

"You bite your tongue, *shipmate!*" the officer said before he could finish. "I suggest you watch who you are talking to. I know how to handle these situations. I went to college."

Everyone in the room laughed, and one said, "Oh god, not one of these."

Even other officers shook their heads. This prick had no idea what he was talking about.

"My name is Ensign Lambert," the officer said. "I did a tour in Afghanistan and am pretty knowledgeable on firearms—"

"Well, *sir*, if you haven't noticed, we don't have any firearms up here, huh?" Boats said. "Can I ask you a question? When you were in Afghanistan, did you encounter any hostilities?"

"No, Petty Officer—since you are not in uniform, what is your name?" Lambert said.

"Just call him Boats, sir," Timmy offered.

Hey, Seaman Recruit Timmy, if I asked for your opinion, then I would ask you," Lambert said. "Otherwise, shut up and mind your own business!"

"Don't talk to him like that," Jose said. "I don't give a rat's ass who you are!" He walked toward the officer, and the officer backed away as if people were going to jump in, but no one did. He was on his own with this one.

"I would not piss him off, sir," Boats said. "He has seen the captain numerous times for punching officers."

Lambert didn't know if it was a bluff or if Boats was serious. He decided to be careful with his choice of words. Looking at Jose, he'd rather not find out the hard way.

He was a young officer fresh out of the academy, like Timmy and Boats and the others a victim to the circumstances. His neat hair combed to the side to hide his receding hairline made it more obvious. Clean, iron-pressed kakis and shiny boots were enough to make Boats hit this pretty boy right in the face. Just a thought he had as he stared him up and down. This guy could not grow facial hair if he tried.

Not one dare embarrass Officer Lambert in front of superior officers and junior sailors alike. He directed his anger towards Boats and Timmy. "When we get rescued, I will put your asses on report for disrespecting a superior officer. Hey, get over here I am talking to you!"

"What makes you think we are going to survive this?" Boats retorted.

He didn't grasp the fact that no one will rescue them. The fact he was even alive was because of his choice not to show up at the XO all-hands in the hangar bay. Instead, he was filing reports on junior sailors. An ass-kisser to his superiors, he hid in his office, making everyone show up while he watched TV. Only when he fell asleep did he hear people running past his office. He yelled, telling them to stop running, but when he looked to his right, he saw what they were running from. He ran with them, pushing his way through the crowd. This little weasel pulled rank to get on the forecastle while others died.

Boats knew this guy had no clue on what has happened the last twenty-four hours. Boats found a quiet space and lay down. He did not want to hear anything more. Just wait. He had no plan, not even ideas.

Lambert walked over. Impatient, he asked Boats, "What do we do now?"

"Nothing. We wait," Boats replied.

"We have to do something," Lambert said. "Excuse me. You two, come here now—hey, where are you going? Why are you not listening to an officer of the United States Navy?"

Boats called them over, saying, "Hey, guys, get with Timmy and Collado. We will post a watch on these doors so no one gets in."

They smiled and walked over to Timmy.

"Why don't they listen to me?" Lambert asked.

"Sir, seriously, stop with the officer crap. Does rank really matter anymore? Look over there. Do you see those chiefs and commanders? Do you see those lieutenants? Every one of them are scared shitless. That's why I am trying to control things up here. We need to have some kind of order. If not, then we would be no better than what is out there."

"I am trying to control—"

"No, sir, you are making things worse. Do you really know what is beyond that door?"

"No, not really? I followed the panic of the crowd. I don't know what they were running from."

"The crewmembers outside those doors are infected! With what? I have no idea, but once you come in contact with the infected, you become one of them, and I assure you, what I saw firsthand you would not like it."

"I don't understand what you mean, Boats."

"You want some advice? Here it is. My chief once told me there are leaders and there are followers. There is no in-between. That is why I am a boatswain's mate. I like to lead. But before you can lead, you have to be a good follower."

The officer just didn't understand as he had this puzzled look on his face.

"Look, sir," Boats continued, "with all due respect, things are different now. People's lives are at stake. Why do you think the other officers in here with us do not want to be in charge? It is a much bigger responsibility no one wants on their hands. I am trying to keep things in control. If there is no control and order, death will win."

While talk was going around with crewmembers, the phone on the forecastle rang. Everyone looked at it. There was a pause and all were quiet, staring at the ringing. Boats yelled, "Someone answer it! I doubt it's the infected calling."

Jose ran to the phone. Boats could not hear who he was talking to but motioned to Jose, silently asking who it was. Jose held up his index finger saying "one second" as the person on the other end was talking to him. He put his hand over the talking end and scanned the room. Pointing at Officer Lambert, he said with a straight face, "Sir, it's the zombies. They want to know if you can meet them in the hangar bay."

Everyone laughed as Lambert was not amused one bit.

"Sir, I am kidding. Boats, it's for you."

Lambert ran to the phone and grabbed it from Jose. With a grin, he whispered, "Stand down, shipmate."

Jose walked away, smirking as if he knew what was going to happen.

"Yes, this is Ensign Lambert. I . . . yes . . . I understand . . . No, I was just—yes . . . A boatswain's mate has been running things up here . . . Understand . . . okay . . . Boats, it's for you."

Boats got up, still stiff from the day's activities. Walking to the phone, he could hear everyone giggling at the officer. Lambert held the phone out. Just as Boats reached for, it he dropped it. Walking away, Boats picked it up and shook his head. "Good evening, sir," he said to the phone. "BM2—"

The pissed off voice who just got done dealing with Officer Lambert cut Boats in the middle of his sentence, "*Sir?* Shipmate, I work for a living! Hello, Boats, this is Master Chief calling from the navigational bridge."

# Chapter 9

## *The Altercation*

Boats smiled as he heard a familiar voice. He remembered Master Chief when Billy first got sick and he called medical. It was good to see he was alive. It was good talking to another salty sailor.

"How many survivors do you have up their, Boats?" Master Chief asked.

"We had twenty but got more, lost a few. We're roughly sixty strong. Others trickled up here," Boats replied.

"I understand. We have all had our losses. It's okay. We tried to escape but was—"

"Shot at, I know. The same thing happened to us. We saw the jets fly and engage earlier. Hey, what did you say to that officer? He looks pissed.

"He remembers me from my last command. I dented his forehead with my navy ring. I thought he was in Afghanistan. I wonder what he is doing here. No matter, he shouldn't be a problem anymore, and if he is, let me know." Master Chief laughed.

"Small navy, Master Chief," Boats said. "What are we going to do?"

"I contacted one of the other ships. They are aware of the infection that our government is trying to contain onboard the ship. That is the reason why there is so much military presence around us. They need our help before they can risk bringing help on board. I don't know how else to say it."

"You have no idea what we went through today. Try me."

"I was reading some of the deck logs and last entries before things got crazy. This guy may be the cause of the virus. Some civilian guy, goes by the name of Billy Gibson. He was one of the reporters that came onboard."

"Oh my god, the guy that threw up all over on the forecastle. I remember him."

"I encountered him just hours before the attack in the hangar bay. He was in the medical bay. He was pretty vicious. I walked on him eating a young female sailor. She turned as well when I was busy keeping him away from me.

"They want his medical records. Everything that was tested on him, and the only way rescue is coming is if we can get all that information for a helicopter that is expecting to arrive tomorrow. No one is going to help us unless we can get this guy's file. They will not approach the infected area unless they know what they are dealing with. Everything is in the medical area. I am up here with civilians and a young female officer and one of your quartermasters. Boats, we need that info!

"I understand, but we do not have any weapons. I only got jerry-rigged weapons."

"If you leave the forecastle on starboard side and go down the AIMD tunnel, cut left down the ladder well, on the port side go through the forward mess decks. Get to the armory. It's opened. There are more than enough weapons inside. Grab only what you can carry."

"Understand. How important is it—"

"It's not a good idea to roam around at night. They seem to be more active. Get some sleep. Hey, Boats, watch out for the big one and smart ones."

"You mean there are more than just runners and jumpers?"

"Jumpers? I have not encountered them yet. But yeah, we encountered a bunch of them earlier. I guess food is getting scarce. This one I saw eating the infected ones. The virus or whatever it was that turned everyone into them is making this one mutate. He ate this one dead crewmember. His muscles from his meat ripped through his skin as he grew. It was kind of freakish. I saw him one other time trying to kill a young girl in the hangar bay. I don't know what the hell she was doing that provoked hundreds of them chasing her. Not a very smart girl—"

Master Chief, she saved our lives. Before we could stop her, she created a diversion so we could lower the RHIB and save others. She was the smartest—"

"I am sorry. I had no idea. She will be in my thoughts. Get some sleep. I will call you in the morning."

Boats hung up. Everyone was around him, wondering what the conversation was about. Boats asked Timmy if the watch rotation on the door was good. Nothing more was mentioned. Boats figured if he said something now, it could cause a panic. Setting his wristwatch, he lay alone.

The several hours that passed seemed only minutes as he sensed someone near him. Opening his eyes, he saw eight pretzel sticks lying near his face on the floor. Getting up, he saw Lambert walk away. Maybe he wasn't all that bad. Just needed direction. Boats smiled at the pretzels and ate his dinner alone.

. . . . .

The sun set over the horizon as darkness engulfed the battlefield. Master Chief wondered why no zombies attacked. All was quiet as the ships around had their navigation lights on. This was the first sign of peace since everything happened two days ago.

The phone rang, but it was not coming from the forecastle, Master Chief answered and heard a female woman crying in agony. "Hello, is . . . anybody there? This is Engineering Third Class Danielle Edingtion!"

Master Chief held the phone about four inches from his ear as she was frantically screaming. "EM3, please calm down," Master Chief said. "Where are you?"

"I am in a female berthing bathroom, please." She cried hysterically. "Please help me!"

"I need you to calm down. Explain to me what happened."

It felt like minutes as there was silence on the other end. The crying ceased, and breathing slowly, she spoke, I was in my rack sleeping when I heard the door slam open. Whoever entered the area was being very loud and disrespectful. Because the lights were out, I couldn't see anything. I kept my curtain shut because I work the midnight shift and people are loud all the time. I sleep in the top rack because I prefer the ventilation, helps me breathe better at night. I remember it was a few minutes and I heard someone, another female, scream. It sounded like she fell out of her rack. There was a struggle as I tried to go back to sleep. A first class petty officer jumped out of her rack. Hearing the commotion, she was going to tell whoever was making a racket to shut the hell up. When she entered the small cubicle area, they attacked her. I heard her struggle, and this woke up others that were sleeping. These things attacked anyone who got out. Seeing what was going on, I peeked out of my curtain and saw one of them on the floor eating someone. Two more joined in the mutilation. They had pulled her out the middle rack while she was asleep. The violent attack was something that I will never forget. My friend who I ate lunch with earlier was lying on the floor with her kidney torn open and her throat slashed open. I saw her! I saw her change into one of them! She lay there still for a few seconds, and then she convulsed, pushing her stomach up, shaking like she was having some sort of seizure. She jumped up and ran into the cubicle across from me and attacked them as well. I got sick and almost threw up. I just stayed quiet until I heard them leave. They went on to the next berthing. These things were just eating people, infecting them." She started crying again.

Master Chief just listened, and when he heard her crying again, he asked her, "Where are you now?"

"I am in a bathroom, in one of the stalls on a phone." She then screamed as Master Chief heard them enter the area. Their snarls and growls could be heard as Master Chief could hear her breathe hard and faster. The doors were broken in one by one as they checked each stall. Breaking each door, they smelled, looking for humans. In the last stall Edingtion had her feet up on the toilet. She saw his dark image in the cracks of the opening and his feet stop at her door. Red blood spatters were on the tiled floor where it stood. It turned and kicked the door open. Edingtion screamed, dropping the phone behind the toilet. The door was pushed on top of her. It was the only thing keeping the infected from biting her. The struggle of her trying to stay alive and the infected trying to kill her was chilling coming from the phone.

The creature pulled the door, jerking it away from her grip. He threw the door against the wall. Master Chief heard the infected turn to her and growled as she tried to fight it off and violently attacked her. It was eating her alive.

Hearing this creature ripping her flesh and enjoying the remains of her carcas was something that would haunt Master Chief in his mind as the sound played over and over.

Sweat ran down his face after hearing what just conspired on the phone. No one else heard what happened. *Better he not tell the two females. It may scare them,* he thought. He then turned to Jenny and Caleigh and decided to change the topic. "I know some of you find this very hard, but if you want to call home, I can give you the outside line. Just don't mention what has happened. Big Navy may be eavesdropping."

Jenny smiled and took Master Chief on his offer. Dialing a code, he punched in the number Jenny gave him, and the phone rang as he handed the phone to her. Pointing at his watch, he held up ten fingers. Jenny knew he meant ten minutes.

"Hello, Ma," Jenny said. "It's me Jenny."

"Oh my god, Jenny, are you okay," her mother asked. "We have not heard from you. We e-mailed you but got no response. What is going on?"

"Um, we're okay. I am doing well. How is Dad?"

"Your dad is fine."

"Can I talk with him?"

"I am sorry. He is not here. He went to the store to get ice cream for . . ."

The slight pause made Jenny think that something was wrong. Listening, she could hear her mother sobbing. "Mom, what's wrong? Are you and Dad okay?"

"Everything . . . is . . ."

"Tell me. What's going on with you two? I don't understand. I thought everything was great between the—"

"Your father and I separated last year . . . I am sorry we lied to you. We were only trying to love and protect you . . . I blame myself."

Master Chief looked over, seeing Jenny cry as her precious glass world was falling apart. Caleigh hugged Jenny, having no idea why she was crying.

"This is not how I wanted you to find out," her mother continued. "I am sorry. I am so proud of you, but his rude comments on your career decisions and . . ."

"So that's it? He never wanted me to join the navy?"

"Honey, he dealt with it because I asked him to. I am sorry I know this is not . . ."

"I love you, Mom. Tell Dad I am sorry for being a disappointment. I wish you would just tell me the—"

"WE TRIED THE BOTH OF US, AND WHAT HAPPENED? YOU REMEMBER WHEN WE TOLD YOU NOT TO BE WITH THAT DEADBEAT PIECE OF SHIT EX OF YOURS? YOU REMEMBER WHAT I HEARD IN THE CAR? I CANNOT DEAL WITH THIS. HE LEFT ME WITH NOTHING. HE LEFT ME WITH NOTHING, JENNY, NOTHING!" With a click, the line went dead.

Jenny dropped the phone crying. Her mother hung up on her. As far as Jenny was concerned, they hated her. Caleigh hugged her, consoling her over the argument she just had. The truth finally came out.

"Maybe we should all get some rest," Master Chief said. "The doors are locked. Nothing should bother us. Besides, it's very quiet tonight, and stars shine brighter than normal. I think it's a good sign."

. . . . .

An explosion and a large flash coming from one of the smaller warships woke everyone sleeping on the bridge. Master Chief grabbed the binos and focused on the action. Hearing repeated gunshots, he heard the ship's horn go off. Then his heart sank as he witnessed one of the ships veer hard port, picking up speed. It was headed directly into the middle of another one of the ships. The collision was imminent as people jumped over the side.

All this was witnessed a few miles away off the right side of the carrier. What happened to cause this horrific accident? Listening to the radio, he could hear the terror of screams and gunfire in the background as it all unfolded. "We sent rescue boats to recover the bodies that were shot earlier near the infected zone of the air craft carrier.. One survivor rescued from a RHIB was extremely hostile . . . attacked crewmembers . . . They were brought onboard . . . infected the crew . . . Warship is over run . . . Three other small ships surrounding the carrier are effected as well . . . . resulted in collision of two US ships . . . Virus not contained . . . Repeat . . . Vir—not—There was static and then silence.

Master Chief turned the radio low so only he could hear. Afraid of how they would react, he did not want to alarm anyone. Shaking his head, he looked outside and saw a huge explosion as two warships collided and took on water. Just then a call came in over the ship's radio. "Warship AIR CRAFT CARRIER, this is SEAL Team Four. Do you copy? Warship, this is SEAL Team Four. ETA 1700. I repeat, ready for pick-up at 1700. Deploy smoke for pickup. Over, SEAL Team Four out."

David walked toward Master Chief, intending to thank him for the daring rescue. Master Chief turned to him and grabbed David by his neck, pushing the back of his head on the glass window and asked, "I want the fucking truth. What the hell happened prior to when you guys arrived in the carrier!"

David knew they may not make it off the ship, so better he tell Master Chief what happened. He began to explain about the job assignment he was sent on and the old man he met in the bar and the military complex and what they discovered in the complex, all the sick people that were held up in the rooms. David explained and detailed the interrogation room and that no one was allowed to leave and all their equipment that was taken because of the break-in.

"Do you know where this area is at on a map?" Master Chief asked.

"We still have satellite access," Andrew said. "There is only a two-hour delay since we are out to sea, but we can find the location."

Zooming out on the map, it took about ten minutes for David to remember landmarks, the local bar. He estimated the trip was seventy-five minutes north in some deep forest. Andrew calculated the approximate area where they broke into the fence.

"There!" David pointed at the area. "Right there is where is it. Zoom in."

Andrew clicked the mouse and it zoomed in, taking a few seconds to focus. At 200 % zoom everyone was in shock of what they saw. There was nothing there. No buildings, no fence, just an empty field. No evidence of a military base.

"No, this can't be right," David said. That's the area where we—"

Master Chief interrupted, "Someone went out of their way to clean up their mess. Since the Internet is up, I will Google the ship and see if anything was mentioned in the news of our whereabouts."

Clicking on U.S. Navy news, he saw that the front cover said "Aircraft Carrier Battle Group Aid in the Nigerian Conflict."

"Well, this is bullshit!" Master Chief said. "This is how things are kept hidden. I guess maybe if the world knew the truth—"

In that instant, the Internet shut off. It was disconnected. It was obvious that very important people were monitoring them at all times.

"I don't think anyone knows what's really happening here," Caleigh said. "How do you cover up an entire carrier? This ship is huge."

"It's quite easy," Jenny replied. "You make it look like an accident."

Master Chief looked at his watch. "Sorry to wake you all. Please go back to sleep. I don't want to hear no more talk of this, okay? Good night."

# Chapter 10

## *THE RED CURTAIN FALLS*

The cold floor was not doing any good for Boat's back. Turning on his side, he heard the phone ringing. He ignored it, thinking that the watch would answer it. A soft female voice then spoke to him, "Boats, the phone is for you."

"What, no late sleepers?" Boats said.

As he looked at his watch, it said 0530. Walking over to the phone, he wiped his face. "Yes, Master Chief, good morning."

"I got some good news and bad news," Master Chief said. "Which do you want to hear first?"

"The bad news."

"We are drifting toward land since the ship was overrun. Andrew, the quartermaster, got the maps out. We need to drop anchor. We are heading for a barrier reef. Not a good situation for a nuclear carrier on foreign grounds."

"Oh, how much time do we have left?"

Master Chief grew silent to gather his thoughts and spoke, "About two days ago we were two hundred miles from land. We are now less than a hundred nautical miles. Now for the good news, we need those files ASAP. A Seal Team will be dropping down to escort our assistance in the rescue operation. I don't know what is out there. We have to have the anchor between 1500 and 1530 today. The area will be about seventy feet to the bottom. After 1530, the current shifts, and we will drift in deeper waters. The Seal Team will meet us at the rendezvous point at 1700 on the flight deck near the smoke flares we will provide."

"I understand. We will get the files first then deal with the anchor. I will handle it, Master Chief, and I know I will keep you informed." Boats hung up the phone and saw everyone sleeping. The peaceful side of his job was when everyone was quiet. He then lightly kicked up Jose and Timmy and walked behind the curtain to discuss the plan, so when everyone woke up, there was no questioning who had what responsibility. As Boats was talking, Mr. Lambert peeked in and wanted in on the meeting. Silence grew, but Boats had no time for his mouth.

0600 came and Boats woke up everyone. Timmy lay out new weapons as Jose prepared to leave the safety of the forecastle. Soon everyone gathered around wondering what the plan was.

Boats began, "I know a lot of you are wondering if we are getting the hell out of here. Let me assure you, we are!" Sigh and smiles appeared on the crowd. "We have to take a small group of us to retrieve some files concerning the first case of this infection, and this was coming from Washington, not me. I will return by 1500, and we must drop the anchor. That means we need to go one deck below and energize the windless to turn on the brakes so the chain don't run, which means we will need people guarding the workers in case of an attack. Everyone, listen please. We will return with firearms.

"Okay, so Jose, Timmy, you're with me. SN Ward, we need you as well. Everyone else stand down until we return from—"

Lambert interrupted, "Boats, I am coming too."

"Sir, I don't think you should."

"No let him come," Jose said. "Zombies gotta eat something. Besides, he may slow them down for us." People laughed.

"That's enough, Collado," Boats said then turned to Lambert. "Okay fine, you want to come? You're more than welcome. You all remember Justine? Don't laugh! This is not funny. Lives are on the line. Okay we got a total of seven of us going. That's a sizeable force.

"Ralph Gibeson, come here!"

A tall Asian gentleman walked toward Boats. He was a newly inducted third class and just got engaged. He was most noted for his extreme workout techniques and toned physical appearance. Boats handed him a line about fifteen feet long. On the end was a ball of line called a monkey's fist. The ball was about a foot in circumference. The monkey's fist had about 100 to 150 sharp screws sticking out about two inches, making the ball looking like a spiked porcupine from hell.

"The line is elastic," Boats said. "Under extreme pressure, it will stretch. Throw it at your enemy and pull. It will do the rest."

"Holy shit! Thanks, Boats," Gibeson said.

"Okay, make sure your skin is covered. Don't let them scratch you or bite you. We believe that's how it travels. We will go covert ops, guys. We don't want to attract attention. Things could go wrong fast, so be alert, and if you get bitten or scratched or ingest blood in your mouth, open wounds, eyes, you're as good as dead."

Lambert had this look of *"what the hell did I get myself into"* on his face. As Collado held the metal door open, he patted Lambert on the back saying, "Sir, safety brief has been conducted. Be safe!"

Boats, Timmy, Lambert, Jose Collado, Ward, Gibeson, and Gunner's Mate Ramos left the forecastle. Closing the door behind them, a cold feeling came. The first passageway was already filled with blood and missing limbs from the attacks. Same as before, walking down the stairs, they got to the AIMD tunnel. There was no infected in the area, only the dead that Boats and Timmy killed earlier. Staring at the door where Justine was last seen before entering the hangar bay, Boats cut left down the ladder well, avoiding the hangar bay. "All clear," the front scouts said as they entered the mess decks going aft.

They quietly walked through the mess decks, and the sa,e sight was all around. Severed body limbs were everywhere as this was once the feeding grounds for the infected. Once-clean floor tiles were now soaked in blood, and you could hear the blood stick to their boots every step they made.

Timmy cracked open the next door, and he scanned the area. He saw nothing but the useless corpse Winston shot earlier leading into the armory area. Boats ran down first, then Lambert, Jose Collado, and everyone else followed. Boats ordered to shut the hatch so they can regroup with live firearms.

Boats posted a watch on either entrance as he scanned the areas. Walking into the office, he saw a phone and called Master Chief to let him know where their location was. Looking in the cabinets, he found walkie-talkie radios also known as Hydras. Calling Master Chief, he tuned in on the same frequency. Now communication was much easier. Looking around the area, Boats told Master Chief over the radio, "Master Chief, calling you on channel 17. Are you there."

"Yes, I hear you loud and clear."

"Great. Uh, we have a problem."

"What is it? Too much guns and ammo and not enough help carrying it all?"

"No, that's the problem. All the weapons, except two shotguns, a pistol, and a dismantled M16, are missing."

"I don't understand. There was about fifty each, including the M240 guns that were mounted on the wall in the back."

"Boats, it's me QM3," Andrew chimed in. "When we left, we counted what was left. It was too much to carry."

"Well, it is all—"

Gibeson interrupted him, "Boats, come here look!"

"What is it?" Master Chief said over the radio. "What is going on?"

"Uh, in the back room, three are dead," Boats replied. "Wait." He turned to his group. "Hey, check them for infections and keep that weapon on its head in case it wakes up.

"What is going on, Boats?" Master Chief asked.

"Uh, these three were shot in the head and in the chest. We checked them and none of them have any indications of the infection. They were not bitten or scratched. WHAT THE FUCK!"

"What? Boats, what is going on!" He could hear everyone get startled on the radio, and something fell.

"Jesus Christ!" Boats cursed. "One of my guys opened up the stand-up lockers, and three more bodies fell out. All were shot, looks like execution style."

"Do you think the infected—" Lambert began before he got cut off.

"No," Boats said. "There was no forced entry. It looks like the living . . . is killing the living."

Everyone froze as all this was processed with what they saw. There was no sign of struggle. The footprints left by the assassins clearly showed this was not done by the infected. Nothing made sense.

Boats called, "Master Chief, we will call you once we get to the medical area. I am turning off the radio. In case you call and we encounter hostiles, the noise will attract them. Over."

Boats checked everywhere for guns and ammo, but whoever was in here cleaned everything. Assembling the M16, Boats grabbed spare parts from other M16 pieces. He knew this was not good. They had only an M16 with three clips, a 9MM with one full clip, and two shotguns with only eighteen shells.

"Hey, Boats," Lambert said. "Can I speak with you?"

Boats walked into the office where Lambert closed the door. Lambert began, "I wasn't honest with you. When I went to Afghanistan, I never really shot a weapon. Uh, I, well, I was there for *admin* purposes only. I was wondering if you could show me how to use the guns." He pulled the pistol out from his pants, pointing it at Boats point-blank range.

"WOAH!" Boats ducked as he swung the gun barrel away from his face. "Are you crazy? Okay, rule one: Don't fucking point that gun at anyone unless you intend to use it, understand? Now this is the 9MM . . ." Boats explained how to load and check the gun as well as chamber the rounds.

A few minutes went by, and the door opened. Everyone stood up, waiting on the next plan since they were all shorthanded on weapons. Boats paced back and forth and looked at his watch. It was already 12:30 pm. "Okay, guys," he said. "We will go up this ladder well then aft down the long passageway straight to medical which will be to our right. We must finish the job. Collado, take the shotgun and nine shells. That's it, and Timmy you take the M16. Ward, take the other shotgun and the remaining shells. Sir, you grab the pistol since that's what you should be more familiar with. Gibeson, you are basically a human weapon. Just don't die, my Asian friend. Gunners mate Ramos, you stay in the middle with me until we get to medical since we both don't have weapons."

Collado said, "Yeah, Bruce Lee will be sad if you die, Gibeson." Everyone laughed.

"Gunner Ramos, did you hear what I fucking said?" Boats said. "You stay in the middle with me until we get to medical since we both don't have weapons. Let's move out. Regulators, move out!"

"Really, are you serious, Boats?" Jose said. "Now we're doing movie quotes? Fucking *Young Guns II*."

They walked up and opened the hatch. The mood was once again quiet as everyone knew how serious things were. They slowly moved and advanced down the passageway. There was not a single infected in sight. The group kept moving.

"How come we have not seen anything?" Lambert whispered.

"I don't care," said Boats. "The less we see of them, the better it is for us. Collado, quietly open the medical door."

As Collado pushed it opened with his gun, he eased and scouted the area. "Looks clear," he signaled.

The end of other hall was another entrance into medical. It was blocked by a barricade of office furniture and medical supplies. Walking halfway down the hall, Timmy hung a left into the surgery room where important medical files may be kept. He separated from the group to find the information and get the hell out of there.

Boats had an idea. Grabbing the huge oxygen bottles, he and Collado set it on a metal tray that was used to put surgery tools on. Strapping it with telephone wire and masking tape, he wheeled it to the entrance. "Okay, Collado, if anything comes, you take the sledgehammer and hit this end as hard as you can. It should propel like a rocket. Here, take the pistol, and once you eye it at a safe distance, shoot the oxygen opening, and we'll take cover."

Lambert handed Collado the pistol, saying, "Damn, Boats. Where did you learn this from?"

Collado interrupted, "He saw this on *SpongeBob squarePants*, sir."

Boats couldn't help but smile. "*Mythbusters*," he said even he thought that was funny. He looked at his watch. "Let's get moving."

A loud scream startled everyone as they looked in the direction of where it was coming from. Running as fast as they could, they rounded the corner, witnessing Timmy throwing shit everywhere, screaming. It was like a child throwing a tantrum. Anything he could grab, he threw, making a lot of noise for others to hear down the hall as well.

"What the hell is wrong?" Boats asked.

"Boats, you better calm him," said Lambert. "He is going to blow our cover!"

"I am, sir. "Timmy, what is going on?"

Giving Boats no time to react, Timmy sucker-punched Boats on the left side of the cheek. It happened so fast, Boats did not see it coming. He lost his balance and fell on his butt. Gaining his balance, he tried to get back up, but Timmy was like a wild man. Lunging back on Boats, he punched him again, grabbing him by his neck. He had Boats pinned on the ground, choking him.

The grip was so tight, Boats could not even talk or gasp for air. He saw tears fall from Timmy's eyes as he hit Boats on the face. Ward and Gibeson heard the commotion and ran in. By the time they went to grab Timmy, Lambert dove, taking Timmy to the floor, trying to restrain him. Timmy sucker-punched Lambert in the nose. He fell back as blood went everywhere. It was apparent Officer Lambert had never been in a fight before.

Ward grabbed Timmy from behind and put him in a chokehold. Boats caught his breath, feeling his throat. He could feel the marks where Timmy dug his nails in. Coughing, he said "What . . . what . . . the . . . hell . . . was that for?"

Timmy stopped fighting. He lay limp and fell to his knees crying. Boats and everyone else in the room had no idea what was going on with Timmy. Ward released the hold as soon as Timmy stopped fighting.

"Hey, talk to me," Boats said again. "What the fuck is wrong?"

"Timmy got up, not saying a word. He grabbed a medical file and threw it at Boats who was sitting on the ground from the scuffle. Looking down at the name on the file, Boats put his hand over his mouth. "Cindy." He opened and read it up. He kept reading, and then he saw it. Looking up at Timmy turning his back, he understood now why he went crazy.

Timmy walked out, not saying a word. The trail of tears was evidence enough that he had reached his breaking point.

Lambert stood up, holding his bloody nose. He walked over to Boats, "What the fuck? Why did we bring him with us if he was going to act like this?"

Boats closed the medical file and pulled Lambert close, whispering in his ear, "Cindy was three weeks pregnant! Jesus Christ!"

· · · · ·

Master Chief looked at his watch, pacing back and forth. David lay asleep from staying up talking to Master Chief all night. Looking at the flight deck, he saw that more of the infected joined the already hungry horde at the base of the island. It looked as if an army was forming outside. The clock said 1300, and he synced it with the ship's time. In the distance, he saw two Raptor fighters approach the ship from the east. As they got closer, he saw three more. A total of ten flew in formation across the carrier. Caleigh was excited as she jumped, clapping for the United States Navy. Master Chief looked at her with a grin. He said, "I know you civilians get excited during air shows, but these are not the Blue Angels. They tried killing us yesterday, so keep it down."

There was another flyby, and the engines roared as one broke hard right from formation. Diving down, his engines whistled as he opened fire on the crippled warships that were burning all night. There was a loud explosion, and a huge fireball of a mushroom cloud was sent into the air. Debris flew everywhere as Master Chief looked at Caleigh's face drop from a smile to fear.

"So this is how they contain the infection?" Jenny said.

"Yes, ma'am, they destroy everything," Master Chief confirmed.

"Why haven't they bombed us?" Caleigh asked.

David awoke, hearing the conversation. "Because we have something they need."

"Once they get the files, and they see we are not infected, the rescue operation should be their primary goal," Jenny said.

A radio beep went on, and Master Chief saw it was Boats calling.

"Hello, Master Chief," Boats transmitted. "Calling on 1, 7, over."

"Go ahead, Boats. What is the status?"

"We are in medical, and we found the files. Billy I think his name was? When that name was mentioned, David and Caleigh perked up.

"Hey, Master Chief," Boats went on, "me and the guys were looking at these files, and before he went under, there is a video file of him talking to one of the nurses concerning how he got infected. He goes on saying that everything about the incident was written on a statement and mailed to his house in the States. Pretty smart if yah ask me."

"Did you see how it started?" Master Chief asked.

"I am no doctor, but it looks like blood activates it. This was a virus, and it goes on saying that all the other hosts were unsuccessful. Uh, blah, blah, reading goes on saying—names some people from Washington were aware of its side effects. They were the money lenders, and because of human experimentation, it had to be done outside the United States."

In the background Lambert spoke, "You mean they knew of this?"

"Not sure," Master Chief replied. "How did you find out all that info, Boats?"

"Well, Lambert here is a computer whiz," said Boats. "We looked in the bag that Billy brought in with him. It was hidden on a memory stick, everything. Images of sick people, a little girl, the latitude and longitude of the location. Looks like he kept a journal. Some guy named Mr. Rene Barrier tried to help them, not sure who this guy is. Here I will read one of many entries.

"Day unknown,

"I am writing to recall the interrogation that we endured. I was brought into a dark room. I could not see anything as I was blindfolded and was beaten because of what we saw at the camp.I refused to say anything. They kept poking me with needles, taking samples of my blood.I recall waking up with an IV in my arm vein.The cold sensation ran through my arm.I could not see anything.I don't know what they injected in me.The next thing I remember I was waking up at the embassy with David and Caleigh.I don't remember much after that.I have been getting sick more than usual, and I didn't tell the others what happened to me.I didn't want Caleigh to worry. Besides, I kind of like her.All pictures and information I mailed home to my address.I have to board the cod that will take us to the carrier.I wish this blood would stop.

"It ends there. I think this is bigger than we thought, huh? Another entry goes

"Day unknown,

"The medication is not working.I am only getting worse. Stomach pains are getting worse. I don't think I can handle this much longer.They said I would get better, but I am only getting worse.I have not slept in days, throwing up blood.Something is wrong;I wish this would all stop.I have to go, will write later if I can even hold a pen.

"Wait, someone is coming . . . I hear someone. Wait, oh my god! We found a survivor!"

"Okay, well, make sure he was not bitten," Master Chief said.

Boats ran to where Ward and Gibeson were. The man lay naked on the floor, his skin pale with the loss of hair and his lips were chapped. His arm rose as if to let everyone know he was alive.

"Get the crewmember on his feet and—" Master Chief began before he got cut off by Boats.

"Uh, I don't think he is one of ours. He is barely alive, and he has a skeleton drinking a bottle with . . . looks like *B* . . . *G.* underneath—"

Master Chief, puzzled, was about to talk when Caleigh screamed. David asked her what was wrong. She said, "It's Billy! And he's alive!"

# Chapter 11

## *THE TAKEOVER*

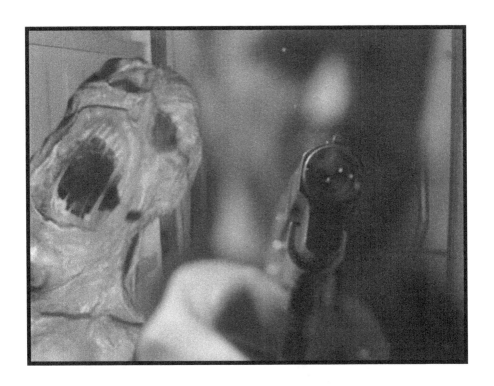

The incident with Timmy put everyone on edge. His quiet moods were making everyone feeling suspicious and edgy. It wasn't until Boats asked that he relinquish his firearm did everyone feel better from the loose cannon they'd suspected him to become. Boats left him alone. It was not good to bother him about the devastating news. Lambert went on to finish copying all the files and photos dealing with Billy on the memory stick.

They stared at Billy. Looking at him lay there on the floor, Ward asked, "What are we going to do with him? He barely looks alive."

Boats replied, "I don't know. I am not a doctor. Besides, look at him. I don't think he can move."

"Hey, Boats, answer the radio!" Master Chief said. "You there, Boats?"

"Yes, I am here."

"He may be the reason this all happened. You better restrain him. I encountered him when he changed. I think you should bring him with us. He may be critical to our rescue."

"He doesn't look like he changed yet. Well, since we have no weapons to carry, we will—

"Oh, and you need to get back to the forecastle. They called me up here looking for you."

"Yeah, we're trying to see how to get him out of here. We need to restrain him or carry him."

"There is something you need to know. When they called on the phone, I heard screaming and gun fire. I tried calling back but the phone is off the hook, and I don't know what is going on up there."

"Well shit, we have no guns up on the forecastle. We came down here to get them in the armory when we found the murdered guys—oh my god!"

Lambert, closing all files, shut the computer off and walked over to where Jose was. The memory stick was in his pocket under safe guard. He was watching Jose sit in a chair, slouched over with his leg propped up on the cart, ready to push at a moment's notice. Everything was quiet and busy dealing with Billy. Walking over to the entrance of the swinging doors, he walked out to stretch. The main hallway was quiet. Looking down the forward part, he saw nothing. He turned around and started to push the door, but something stopped him.

There was a running infected, and he could see more of them come down the ladder well on the aft mess decks, hooking a left away from them. They were still a good distance away. His curiosity got the best of him as he looked back through the small window doors and saw Jose still sitting.

Lambert kept walking, keeping his back against the wall, getting braver as the horde still did not see him. Since the evacuation from his office, he never really saw one up close. Tiptoeing, he approached. He counted over fifty running and scurrying and heading aft in a hurry. Their food was scarce, and they must have been scavenging. The line of the infected was getting less and less as they went on their business. Standing only fifty feet from the ladder, Lambert decided to retreat to the medical area where everyone was.

Turning around, he saw that one was standing at the other end of the hall, staring at him. Lambert froze in panic. Realizing he and the infected was about even with the door leading into the medical door, he inched his foot forward slightly. The zombie moved his foot forward one step as well. Lambert knew he fucked up. It was going be a race to the door. And this one was daring him to run. He took another step, and the zombie mimicked as well. Lambert reached for his pistol then realized Jose had it. "Okay, you want to play? Let's play," he said staring at the dead. Four more appeared behind that one zombie. Now the tables were not in Lambert's favor as he was clearly outnumbered.

The loud roar from the infected was like a gun going off at a race, and he ran as fast as he could. Running a full sprint, the zombie ran like a mad man swinging its arms, spewing blood. Lambert got to the door as the infected headed right for him. Looking at its face, Lambert was scared to death. Itss right upper lip was ripped completely off. Its right cheek was severely cut open, exposing his lower jawbone and teeth. Its skin looked like some rotten decay as its joints cracked. The infected had white fungus growing around where his eyes once were.

Just seconds before it reached him, Lambert swung the door, hitting the zombie in the face. Everyone looked in the direction, pointing their guns at the entrance. Lambert ran right behind Jose, screaming at him to give him the pistol. The first one entered, and as soon as it appeared, Jose popped his head off. Three more entered, and all were laid to rest at the hands of Jose.

"What the hell is your problem?" Jose said. "You asshole, you're going to get us all killed!"

"GIVE ME YOUR GUN!" Lambert shouted. "I ORDER YOU TO GIVE ME YOUR GUN!"

"You better get the fuck away from me, or I will throw you out there!" Jose said.

There was another confrontation, and Jose jumped up, grabbing Lambert by the back of his collar and behind his pants. He picked him up and walked him out to the doors. Just as he was about to drop him, hundreds of them from both directions were coming. The noise sounded like a stampede from both directions.

"Shit, we are trapped!" Jose said and threwLambert back into the room. "You fucking idiot, you fucking led them right to us!"

Lambert was flung on the floor like a rag doll. Getting up, he ran to find Boats. He was nowhere to be found. A scuffling noise was coming from the back as he ran to the blocked entrance. He saw Boats, Gibeson, and Ward trying to move the the stuff that blocked entrance as fast as possible. Since the other way was blocked with the horde coming from both directions, this was the only would be the only way out.

Chairs, table pieces, beds, and cabinets were all thrown across the room as they all frantically moved. As Boats moved the chair, throwing it across the room, Lambert just stood there. The end piece of a deck was stuck as Boats could not move it. Trying to push with his back against it, he dropped his legs and started to push up, but it was not budging. A few seconds later, it finally moved and fell off the pile. Looking at how the big office piece moved, Lambert saw that Timmy was the reason it moved so easily. Holding his hand out, Boats said, "What the hell you doing sitting down? Let's get the hell out of here!

"Huh, you okay Boats?" Timmy said. "Sorry about the shiner."

"It's okay," Boats replied. "I understand and I am sorry, um, for . . . well . . . you know."

"Now is not the time," Timmy said. "Let's keep moving this stuff. I think we can get the door open. Lambert, you gonna stand there or help us?"

"So how did they know we were here, Lambert?" Boats asked.

"I . . . I . . . don't know," Lambert stammered. "I think Jose made some noise and they heard him. I honestly don't know."

"Well, we don't have time for the finger-pointing. Help us get out of here before we become dinner for one of them."

Jose waited with his hand on the sledgehammer, ready to come down on the oxygen knob end fitting. The ground shook as something big was coming. He could hear them, the loud screams as they approached, but something much larger was coming. Opening the door, it entered, the monster that killed Justine. This thing was *huge*! It had to bend down just to fit in the entrance. As a small zombie tried to sneak through its legs, this thing grabbed that zombie, and with one bite, it ripped him in two. It roared as this was the first time this one ate its own kind.

"JESUS CHRIST!" Jose shouted. "GET OUT OF HERE, EVERYONE! I DON'T KNOW IF I CAN HOLD THIS ONE!" With a large swing, he hit the oxygen bottle, busting the fitting end completely off. The amount of pressure made the bottle and the table it was tied on into a rocket. As it picked up speed, the white whizz of the air escaping could be seen. It hit the freak, knocking him off his feet. The creature fell back about ten feet into the wall. Dazed, it tried to get back up, but the bottle still had some pressure. Jose reached with his pistol, and aiming with one eye shut while the other eye looked down the sight, he fired. The bullet cracked as it headed for the cylinder. It hit the bottle, and the spark was enough to cause the chain reaction for the explosion.

A fireball engulfed the air and anything that was affected with pure oxygen. The heat was tremendous as zombie pieces of burned flesh went flying everywhere. The loud fireball spread out in all directions the zombies were coming from. The loud thunderous roar shook the place.

The smoke filled the area and small fires ignited, and Jose was knocked back. He tried to get his bearings while his ears were ringing. The sounds of the horde screaming from burning to death was deafening to his ears. One ran in, completely engulfed with fire. You could hear the skin boiling as he still tried to find human flesh. Immediately, Gibeson ran into the room to see what the explosion was. He could see fire zombies starting to enter the room. Pulling out his spiked ball, he decided to give the others some time to escape. Gibeson whistled as the fire zombie looked in his direction. The monkey's fist ball was thrown into his face.

Gibeson wrapped his hands three times around the line then pulled. Skin and burnt flesh ripped off his face as the fire zombie screamed in pain. He swung the weapon on his right side, and it made a whistling sound. The faster he swung, the faster it whipped, increasing the whistling sound. About four more entered, surrounding Gibeson. He kept turning so they could not take him from behind. Another five more came in. Gibeson was now surrounded by about twelve of them. They snarled and screamed at him, keeping a distance from the weapon being swung. At the corner of his eye, he could see Jose trying to get back on his feet.

The first fire zombie dared his bluff and charged head in on for his throat. Gibeson threw the spiked ball right in his face as hard as he could with the momentum gained from the whipping. It struck the infected right in his face, busting what was left of his rotten teeth. Another attacked from behind. Gibeson heard the clumsy creature coming. He pulled the spiked ball as hard as he could, ripping it out of the first attacker's face then ducking with cat like reflexes. The ball of death flew over Gibeson, hitting the other one in the face. He ran right into it. The image looked as if he was running and someone swung with a baseball bat. Gibeson grabbed the ball and back in the swinging form. Two more charged this time from his side. He swung the line around his own neck. As the ball circled his neck two times, he kicked one in the chest. He then turned around, making the ball go in the other direction, unraveling it off of him neck and hitting the other one on the side. Two more charged at the same time. One from the front, the other from behind. Gibeson ran toward the one in front of him, wrapping the line three times around the zombie's neck. He then turned 180 degrees and wrapped the other line around the other one. He pulled, and the two were forced together, all tied up. He then pulled the line as hard as he could, severing their heads, and as the ball of death approached, it finished the job of severing their heads off.

There was no rest as the remainder of them was after him. He ducked, flipping one over his back, roundhouse-kicking the other right in the face. As he saw the last one, he noticed him wearing a TLD, and he remembered Boats talking about these "smart ones." The creature walked slowly towards Gibeson, making him slowly step back. Gibeson was waiting for him to make the first move. The tense standoff was beyond anything he encountered before. This was a fight for his life. A few seconds after the smart one crept slowly toward him, it just stood up and walked away. Gibeson was puzzled and took this as a win.

"WHAT?" Gibeson shouted. "YOU GONNA WALK AWAY? YOU FUCK! YOU SCARED—"

There was a sharp crush on Gibeson's ankle, and he fell to the ground. He looked at the pain and saw a crawler gnawing at his leg. He realized this smart one had no intentions on having contact with him. Instead, he distracted him as the other zombie slowly waited to grab him for the trap. Four more jumped on him. Ripping his stomach open, they feasted on his organs. Soon the horde's feeding frenzy was on him as more rushed in the room.

Gibeson was still alive as he saw his stomach get thrown out. He could feel everything as he screamed in pain. These creatures craved blood as they ate, spitting chunks and flesh everywhere. His skin was ripped off to get to the muscles.

Jose witnessed this as he got to his feet. He could not believe how ruthless these creatures were. From his vantage, he could hear Boats and the others trying to escape. Still they were not out of the area yet. Jose knew they would need more time. He wondered for a time how all this unfolded, then he remembered Lambert running in the door with the infected. Jose Collado screamed, "LAMBERT, I SWEAR IF I DON'T MAKE IT THROUGH THIS, I WILL COME BACK AS ONE OF THEM AND PERSONNALY FIND AND KILL YOU!"

It was the last words spoken from Collado. The remaining survivors focused on Lambert. He knew this was his fault, and rather than say anything, he frantically started moving the rest of the debris blocking their escape route.

"GOT IT," Timmy shouted. "We can get through! I got the damn door open!" The opening was only three feet. Timmy popped his head left and right. All clear. There was no sign of any of them. They pulled the door open, and Ward, Boats, and Lambert carried Billy who was not conscious of anything. Once everyone squeezed through, Timmy was the last one through. On the other side, Boats pushed the door enough for him to escape. As Timmy slid through, he looked back as saw hundreds of them fill up into the room looking for food. He knew Jose and Gibeson were not going to make it. These things rampaged through everything, knocking stuff over, growling, snarling, licking up blood on the floor.

Boats shut the door as the debris fell on the other side, assuring that the door stayed blocked. He could hear the infected smelling human odor, but they could not comprehend where they went.

"We can take turns carrying this guy," Timmy said. "If we stay along the port side, we should avoid them. Just don't go near the hangar bay!"

"Good idea," Boats said. "Anyone with weapons, go about fifteen feet ahead. We will need scouts. These things are active now."

Understanding how dangerous things got, Ward and Lambert went ahead. Armed with the shotgun and a pistol with only five bullets left, they advanced toward the front.

"All clear." Lambert announced. "We will go up this ladder well back into the tunnel and back up to the forecastle."

The tunnel was clear, with the already slain zombies strewn around. They went up the ladder well on to the door that led to the forecastle. Boats knocked on the door and waited. No answer. He knocked again. "Hey, guys, open the fucking door. We're not them! Open up!"

"Hey, guys, open up!" Lambert said.

The handles unlatched, and the door opened. Boats walked in carrying Billy. Looking around, he saw everyone sitting on the flood Indian style with their hands bound behind their backs. Walking through, he felt the end of a gun pressed on his head. He then heard the safety unclick and a voice say, "Don't fucking move or say a word, or I will blow your goddamn head off!"

# Chapter 12

## THE EXCUSE FOR MUTINY

Boats froze as the others behind him had no idea what he was doing. The voice spoke, "How many of them are you?" Boats held up four fingers. The voice said," How many are armed?" Boats held up two fingers. The voice spoke, "Tell them to unarm and throw their weapons inside."

Boats answered, "I cannot do that. If those things come, they will not have a fighting chance."

"Hey, Boats, what's the hold up?" Timmy called. He had no idea why Boats was not answering him.

"Hey, guys, when you enter," Boats said, "no Clint Eastwood shit, okay? This guy got a gun to my head. I am fine, just no sudden movements."

The others didn't understand as they slowly entered. Soon all were facing guns pointed at them. The unknown soldiers closed the door and one stood in case any of the infected got near.

"What the hell is going on here?" Lambert began. "I demand—"

"Hey, Lambert," Timmy said, "now is not the time you use rank."

"Who are you guys?" Boats asked.

The voice spoke, "I am Airman Hutchington. Well, I was. Now things are all different, but you can call me Hutch for short."

"Nice to meet you," said Boats. "This is Timmy, Officer Lambert, Seaman Ward, and we found this survivor."

"Jesus, is he even alive?" Hutch said. "Shit, he looks infected! KILL HIM!"

"No, no, he is not," Boats said. "We need him alive."

"Why do you need him alive?"

But Boats realized that if he told him the truth, they may use Billy as leverage for their own gain. Looking around, he found all the guns and ammo that was missing. About twenty of them were armed to the teeth and had ski masks on, to hide what horrific deeds they did. Pointing their guns, the group surrounded Boats and his team. They acted more like gorilla militia. Hutch must have been the leader.

"We went to the armory and saw the bodies. What happened?" Boats asked instead.

"You remember what the skipper said?" said Hutch. "Every man for himself. Well, we refused to surrender. Once we armed up, some tried to stop us."

"Stop you from killing the zombies?" Timmy asked.

"No, I told them the new plan," Hutch replied, "kill everything, the dead, the living. Better to kill them fuckers before they turned. Some refused to help us, so we did them a favor."

"You guys seriously have some issues you have to deal with," Lambert said.

"What did you say? *No*, I will tell you that we only wanted to live, not conform to orders anymore. I didn't sign up for this shit!"

"You guys are crazy!" Timmy said. "I can't believe the rest of you following this guy!"

"No, we are going to survive until we either kill everyone or they kill us," Hutch replied. "We saw the other ships attack some trying to escape. How do you think that makes us feel? Our country killing its own? They are no better than those infected!"

"That don't give you guys the right to take judgment on the living!" Boats said.

"Hey, don't give me the fucking speech," Hutch said. "I asked you a question. What the hell is this guy doing with you?" He pointed his gun at Billy.

"We thought he might need help," Timmy replied. "That's all."

"Listen," Lambert offered. "Maybe we can work this out like civilized human beings."

"Who the fuck are you?" Hutch turned his gun on Lambert. "Some officer? That don't mean shit now. I should bore a bullet in your head right now! Guys, take their fucking weapons or shoot them! I am done fucking with them!"

As they tried to grab their weapons, Ward and Lambert pointed their guns at them, and they reacted by pointing all their guns at them. It was the scene of who was going to shoot first.

"Okay, everyone, calm down," said Boats. "Everyone, slowly put your weapons down. Ward, Lambert, calm down, seriously clam the fuck down."

"You remember when you told me don't point it at anything unless your intentions are to fire?" Lambert said. "I am gonna—"

"Lambert, calm down please," Boats said. "Put your weapons down. This is no time for a shootout. We are all pointing guns at each other. The enemy is out there, not in here! Now, everyone, calm the fuck down!"

Ward and Lambert slowly lowered their guns. The soldiers took their guns from them and threw them in a pile. They were forced to put their hands over their heads.

"Okay, Boats," Hutch said, "since you seem to be in charge here, let me explain how this is going to work. And this goes for everyone! If you are not with our cause, then you are one of them. I ask you all! Boats, maybe its best you talk to your group since they listen only to you."

"I cannot force them to do anything." Boats shookhis head.

"I was afraid you were going to say that." Hutch pointed at one of his followers, and they randomly grabbed one of the guys in the group. He was a Hispanic petty officer first class. Putting him on his knees, Hutch pointed the 9MM at the back of his head. "I am going to ask you nicely. Talk to your group." He clicked the safety off.

Boats bowed his head, not saying anything. In a split second, Hutch pulled the trigger, and the bullet splattered the sailor's brains all over the floor. He fell flat on his face as blood rushed out the entrance wound. The horror of what enfolded was surreal. The other's started to cry and plea.

Boats stood up and nodded. This guy was not one to call a bluff. He was put into a situation where if he figured he lie, this psycho would either spare their lives or kill everyone. Looking at his watch, he realized that time was running out to drop the anchor and meet the rescue team. He did not want them knowing anything. Better he not say anything to make them suspect anything.

It was then that Boats noticed Hutch pull out a small knife from his back pocket. Lifting up his left sleeve, he cut himself a small slash, about two inches. There were many of these cuts up and down his arm. Boats counted about thirty or more before he covered them up. It kind of made sense, like a light switch going on in Boat's head. This kid kept record of how many killings he acted out. Each slash was a victim. *How did he get into the navy? He is a fucking nutcase,* Boats thought. *Better to reason with him than get him pissed off.*

"Okay, fine," Boats said. "I will talk to them. No more killing, okay?"

"Fine," Hutch agreed. I will keep my word for now, but give me reason to doubt your intentions, and I will fucking kill them all! I don't give a shit. I have nothing to lose!"

Walking away, he sat forward of the forecastle, cleaning his M16. Boats went behind one of the curtain with some of the trusted guys. Hutch ordered one of the masked men to monitor them at all times. As Timmy, Ward, and Lambert walked back there, one of the soldiers followed and took off his mask.

"Holy shit! Brandon Drew?" Boats said. "Didn't you work in deck in our sister division? Why are you with this psycho?"

"Guys, trust me," Drew said. "It is not by choice. I didn't have a *fucking* choice. He was going to kill me if I didn't help him. This guy is a loose cannon!"

"How did he get this . . . well, you know . . . crazy?" Lambert asked.

"Okay, listen up, and I have to speak low because if he suspects I am telling you, he won't think twice killing me. Everyone, listen up," Drew said.

Drew was a native from Boston. His accent was distinct. His short crew cut gave him that young look. But he was a workout machine, always staying in shape. He was also a short-tempered Irish kid, but he was very street smart. He explained what happened. "During the initial attack in the hangar bay, there were about thirty of us that escaped in a space. The chiefs and officers were in charge. In the beginning, we had no problem listening to them. Then one of the chiefs had this idea to go to the armory. That was where we all headed, about thirty deep. How we were not noticed by the infected was pure luck, or so we thought. So once we got down there, we saw four of them already dead. I guess some survivors had the same idea. We closed the hatch and armed up. This is when things got crazy. So we all armed up, and this chief and some commander—shit, I forgot his name—ordered the junior guys up the hatch first. They went up one by one, and there was an ambush. The infected were waiting for them to come up. If we had a grenade, we could have cleared the area out. But we don't carry those kinds of weapons on board. When the seaman, airman, and engineman popped their heads up, the zombies grabbed them and pulled them up by force, infecting them. Some were eaten. Others were infected. Some body parts were thrown back down the hatch, daring more to come out.

"This chief and these officers didn't have a plan or a clue how to stop the killings. Instead they were sending everyone to their bloody graves. There was talk in the back of the ranks about standing up to them. This guy Hutch was ordered by the chiefs and officers to go next. He refused and they forced him, screaming at him. He stood his ground, and when the chief put his hands on him, two more officers pointed their guns at Hutch. He was ordered up the ladder well to the hatch opening. Hutch put his M16 down and pulled out his pistol from behind and killed them. He only injured the chief, shooting him in the shoulder. I think it was the right shoulder. Hutch ordered the others to take his gun. The chief, in shock, fell back. The other officers tried to grab Hutch's gun but, he was much quicker, ending their lives as well. All of their guns were taken by force as well. Other junior sailors joined in the mutiny in fear of being shot or being killed by the infected. After that, I watched in disbelief as Hutch ordered at gunpoint to make the chief go up the hatch. I remember seeing this grown man cry and plea for his life. How the tables have turned! He peeked up, and one of them bit his head off, and his body fell back down the ladder well. Hutch decided to wait it out, you know, until they leave. And eventually after a few hours, I guess they got bored and moved on. But while we were down there, some petty officers did not agree with Hutch and were trying to pull rank on him. They were executed immediately. That's when he took charge of all the weapons and ammo. Those who refused to help him, he killed. Hutch snapped, and there was no turning back as he was aware of his actions. We left the armory and started opening up spaces where we saw survivors. He offered them to follow him, and when they said no, he ordered them killed. On the way, we encountered some of the creepers, and that's when he killed anything—living and the dead. He just stopped sorting the living and dead. He went on saying that if the living survived, they would eventually be hunted by the infected and would turn. This was the fear he planted in those who followed him. He offered them salvation, but when they questioned his motives, he killed them. That's why I had no choice."

"How many did you kill?" Boats asked.

"No one," Drew replied. "When the slaughter happened in the armory, I acted like my gun was jammed or couldn't fire. So far, it's worked. But I didn't think twice killing the infected."

Boats listened as much as he could to gather as much information and realized this guy was pushed to the point that he honestly thought he was doing the right thing.

"Well, Drew, where do you stand in all this?" Timmy asked.

"I am not with this crazy fuck," Drew replied. "I had no choice, Boats. He executed a lot of survivors, and the only reason why no one has challenged them is he promised them a way out of here, so now he has followers."

"Well, we are running out of time," Boats said

"What do you mean?" Drew asked.

"Never mind, Drew." Boats turned to Timmy. "Timmy, you are going to have to get out of here and contact Master Chief on the bridge. It's suicide, I know, but it's the only way. Lambert, Timmy is going to need a distraction."

"What should I do?" Lambert asked.

"Do what you do best. Be yourself," said Boats.

"Hell, no! This guy will not think twice to kill me," Lambert said.

"They have the upper hand," Timmy put in. "They have all our guns."

"Leave that to me," Boats said. "I have an idea."

Walking out of the curtain, Drew put his mask back on and followed. He explained to Hutch that it would best to send a small scout to find an escape route. Hutch was not buying it. Boats insisted that his guys survived this long and offered that if some of his guys went, then one of his soldiers went with him. This was enough to allow the plan to work.

Timmy left with the radio, along with Drew and Ward. Their plan was to act as if they were looking for an escape route, but instead contact Master Chief and get some more guns or firepower out here.

"Boats, you better not be trying any sneaky shit because I don't have time for games," Hutch warned.

"Look, we all want to get out of here," Boats said. "They will call us on the phone once they find a way out."

Timmy, Ward, and Drew left the forecastle and went into the nearest berthing where the deck guys once lived. Drew took his mask off and Timmy ran to the phone while Drew and Ward stood watch.

"Hello, is this Master Chief?" Timmy said.

"No, I am sorry this is Caleigh," came the response. "Master Chief is concerned as the horde is trying to get to find a way up to us."

"FUCK! Tell Master Chief that he needs to call me as soon as possible."

"Okay, I—wait. Hold on. Here he is."

"Boats, what's the word?" Master Chief asked.

"This is Seaman Timmy. Uh, we have a problem on the forecastle. The guys up there have been taken hostage, and this crazy guy just killed a sailor that wasn't infected. He was saying that if they didn't follow him, he would kill them all."

"Where is Boats?"

"He convinced Hutch to let three of us go to find an escape route. But our main job was to call you."

"We missed the window for dropping the anchor, but we cannot miss the rescue. Timmy, open both ways to the forecastle. Lead them in and get as many as you can to escape out the other way."

"Are you serious? You want me to—"

"Do you have the files? And Billy, is he still with you guys?"

"Yes, Lambert has the file, and Billy is still not waking up. I don't understand. He has not responded to anything. He is with us."

"I know how crazy this sounds, but you have to trust me. Let them in. Let the horde take care of them all. You need a distraction and the horde will create the perfect alibi. Rescue anyone you can. You have thirty minutes before our window closes. Estimated time of arrival for the rescue is 1700, and its 1630 now."

"I understand. I will handle it. See you at the pickup spot." Timmy hunging up the phone. He had this expression as if he was going to be sick to his stomach. Drew and Ward wanted to know what was said. Timmy put his hands on his head. "Guys, we have to go to the hangar bay."

"Are you crazy?" Ward said. "The infected are there."

"Shouldn't we ignore that area?" Drew put in.

"We will have to use the infected in order to save lives," Timmy said.

"The needs of the few outweigh the needs of the many," said Ward.

# Chapter 13

## *THE ENEMY OF MY ENEMY IS MY FRIEND*

Master Chief realized he had much of the guns and ammo in the extra bags they brought. Now a plan must be devised to get off the bridge and onto the flight deck, but that was going to be easier said than done. Looking in the offices on the eighth level, Master Chief found some line used for hoisting up flags. Cutting and doubling up the line, he made a makeshift line to climb down.

"Okay, guys, we will wait until 1650, about 10 minutes before the chopper arrives, then we will climb down," he said.

"What about the infected that are surrounding the flight deck near the base of the island?" Jenny asked.

"We will have to blow our way through," Master Chief replied. "I told the other guys the plan to be up here at 1700, so I will wait up here to give them cover fire. I don't know how bad this is going to be, but they will be bringing up a lot of infected. We just have to prepare."

"Well, I can help if you need me, Master Chief," David said.

"They will need all the help they can get. Andrew, help me check these knots. Make sure they don't slip. It's a long way down."

. . . . .

Timmy devised an idea. This was the only way. Ward would stand by the port entrance door, and Drew would stand by the starboard door. Timmy then got to a phone and called Boats. The phone was back on the receiver.

"Hello, is Boats there?" Timmy said.

"Hey, man," Boats whispered. "I have to talk like there is an escape so bear with me. Hutch is looking right at me."

"Okay, here is the plan. Get all the survivors to the port side, and when we enter the starboard side, have everyone duck. Wait until the soldiers are busy shooting and we have Ward on the other side. He will open the door, make sure the guard on the port side is distracted. We will make a run to the flight deck. We are going to try to go up and over to avoid the hangar bay."

"I don't understand," Boats said.

"Listen to me," said Timmy. "In order to deal with these guys and get the files and Billy and most of the survivors out before the rescue, I am going to bring them up to the forecastle."

"Bring who? Who are you going to bring?"

The infected, most of them. It's the only way. Keep everyone away from the starboard entrance. Once you hear the knock, be ready.

"SHIT! Oh my god are you—Yes"—he looked at Hutch—"okay, rescue will be coming from the starboard side." He said out loud.

Hutch smiled, having no idea what was going to happen in ten minutes' time. He bragged to his soldiers, assuring that he was going to get everyone who followed him to safety.

Timmy then hung up the phone and headed to the hangar bay. Opening the double doors, he remembered that the last time he was here was when they attempted to get the RHIB. He looked and saw hundreds, maybe about a thousand, of them walking, looking for food. They walked slowly as if they were preserving their energy for the hunt. His palms were sweating as he knew only ten minutes remained. "This has got to be the stupidest fucking stunt I ever attempted," he said, and making the sign of the cross, he ran into the hangar bay firing his gun into the air.

The horde now stronger in numbers looked at the living guy running and went for him. They fell for the bait. Timmy ran as fast as he could, screaming and shooting his gun and making as much noise as possible. He made it to the middle point of Hangar Bay II when the rest of the horde ran from Hangar Bay III to kill him.

He cut to his right as two zombies were in his path. He shot one in the leg, the other in the face. Jumping over them like a hurdle, he had all of them behind him. Every zombie in all three hangar bays was chasing him. It was a narrow path before he could enter the tunnel that led up to the forecastle. There were only fifty feet more when four smart ones blocked his path. Aiming his pistol, he shot, but these ones moved before he could get a shot off. Timmy realized he was wasting shots. His path was blocked, so he cut port side to the left and ran up the side ladders. He had no choice as all the other ways were blocked. The horde multiplied into the thousands and was following him. The howls and grunts drowned the environment with shrills of terror. These things were hot on his trail. Timmy ran up another ladder well as fast as he could, skipping steps and running forward.

"WARD! WARD!" Timmy shouted. "KNOCK! KNOCK! THEY ARE ALL COMING! SHIT, HURRY!

Ward banged on the door as hard as he could.

Boats convinced Hutch to put everyone on the port side of the forecastle. His excuse was questioned by Hutch. "Why do we have to move everyone over there? I don't understand why."

The loyal soldiers pointed their weapons, and the sailors held hostage were forced on their feet and moved to the port side. Once everyone settled back down, Boats looked at his watch, wondering when this suicide plan was going to work. Hutch walked up to the scared people and pointed his gun at the head of one of sailors. Looking at Boats, he was growing, annoyed and wanted everyone to know he was not one to be fucked with. As he cocked the pin back, the interruption of Ward banging on the door distracted him, and he looked at the door.

Boats didn't get it at first. He knew what Timmy said. Get everyone on the port side, and they would knock on the starboard side, but now the loud banging was coming from the port side. Unless something went wrong and he had no choice, he realized the horde was coming up the port side.

"EVERYONE, GET TO THE STARBOARD SIDE! RUN!" Boats bellowed.

Hutch witnessed everyone running and listening to Boats in a panic. In a desperate order to control the crowd that was screaming, he ordered his soldiers to open fire. The soldiers did what they were told as bullets ripped through the sailors, making some fall. Others were killed instantly. Ward was banging on the door, but the soldier that was guarding the door was too busy shooting the sailors.

Lambert heard the constant banging and looked for Boats. He was under fire. He would have to make the choice. If he didn't get that door open, Hutch would kill everyone anyway. It now was his choice. He didn't think twice. He ran for the guard by the port door and slugged him in the face. The guard didn't see it coming. He was blindsided, too busy killing his fellow shipmates.

Hutch saw Ensign Lambert assault his soldier. He aimed his M16 at Lambert and fired. The bullet hit Lambert in his back. He fell to his knees. Hutch focused on killing others as he saw Lambert fall to the ground. Now everyone was defenseless. Lambert looked up. He was next to the door. He crawled, pulling on the handles and unlatching them one at a time. Pulling himself up, he grabbed the last lock and hung on it until it unlatched. The door swung open, and Ward and Timmy ran through. Timmy flung the door open. Lambert was not expecting to get hit with it. He flew back about ten feet on his back and slid on the hard floor. Timmy ran to help him and saw blood leaking on the floor. "Oh my god, Lambert, you've been hit!"

"I . . . I am sorry for everything," Lambert said.

"Hey, it's okay. We need to take you—"

"No, leave me. I can't feel my legs."

"Oh my god, did I do that?"

"No, Hutch shot me in the back. He may have hit my spine, I . . . I *cannot feel my legs*. He cried.

Timmy could hear them coming. The infected were in hot pursuit.

"Here is the memory stick," Lambert said. "Take it. Make sure Master Chief gets it. You tell that son of a bitch I am sorry for everything. Now give me your pistol."

Timmy took the memory stick, which was covered in blood. He held Lambert's hand and put the pistol in his hand, nodding his head.

"I am sorry about Cindy, I heard she was expecting . . . Please forgive me. Now get the hell out of here! Go, before I change my mind!" Lambert said. He lay on the ground watching everything unfold, thinking to himself what Boats said about trying to keep order and discipline, if not we were no better than the dead.

Timmy got up and ran to Boats. He got to the door as the horde entered the port side entrance. Boats and Timmy grabbed as much guns as they could carry. The infected was starting to fill up the forecastle, and the soldiers were blindsided. They were laughing as they shot the innocent survivors. Then an infected jumped on one of them, scratching his throat wide open. It was too late. The horde was here. Hundreds of them filed in, invading the forecastle. Slashing and biting, they fed on the soldiers and the survivors. Boats, Timmy with Billy in his arms, Ward, and Drew escaped with only about ten survivors from the starboard side. On the way out, Boats and the small survivors grabbed any weapon they could carry. There was so much mass confusion that Hutch didn't know what to shoot. The soldiers looked at Hutch for answers on how things got so fucked up, but he could not do anything but accept his fate.

Boats shut the door, and they could hear the cries of hundreds of them as they feasted and ate. It did not matter how many guns there were. When they tried to reload, they were mutilated. There was faint roar as even Hutch was attacked. These zombies had no intentions on creating more of the infected. They were hungry and wanted to feed only.

Boats ran down the small passageway and attempted to go up the ladders to get to the flight deck. Zombies came from up top, running down. Hearing all the gunshots, they got excited and more followed. The only way was down and find another escape route.

"Save your ammo," Boats ordered. "We will need every shot!"

They ran down the ladder well, cut to the right, then back in the tunnel. There was no time to wait. They had only five minutes until the rescue. They ran into the hangar bay. It was still infected with some creepers. But they kept it tight. Running, Drew and Ward aimed for the heads. Boats and Timmy held on to Billy. Some of the other survivors took arms, helping out where they could. Making it to Hangar Bay II, they cut left up the ladder well. The jumpers waited in ambush, grabbing some of the survivors, thinning out the group.

Creepers in each space were laid to rest as they made their way up. On the next level, more approached. Ward shot their heads at point-blank range. There were only two more levels to go. Five waited on the top as Drew made his shots count. They dropped. Boats and Timmy were still carrying Billy who was unconscious. They quickly stepped over the dead as they could hear hundreds of them coming up the ladder well.

Drew was watching their back with his gun pointed at the horde behind them. He stepped over the ones he shot, but one of them grabbed his leg, holding him in place. Drew screamed and shot him in the back of the head. When he looked to see where the rest went, one of the infected grabbed his shirt and pulled him violently down the ladder well right into the feeding frenzy.

"What happened to Drew?" Boats asked.

"SHIT! WE LOST HIM!" Timmy shouted back. "Keep going! We're almost to the flight deck."

Four more waited on top. Boats laid Billy down for a second as he grabbed his pistol and shot them. Two times in the head.

"Why did you shoot them twice?" Timmy asked.

"Double tap, bitch!" Boats replied. "Keep going! We got less than two minutes!"

When they opened up the door to the flight deck, they discovered that hundreds of them waited for them. They were all looking up at the bridge. Timmy slammed the door shut.

"Shit, we can't go that way! Here try this exit!" Timmy suggested.

Boats opened the other side, but there were more of the infected. He had no choice. he opened fire to make a path.

Master Chief heard the guns going off and knew this was the signal. Everyone knew their jobs once they got to the flight deck. This was going to be a war! The line dropped, and Master Chief and David started shooting from up top. Blood spewed everywhere as the zombies fell. The automatic fire hit their heads easily from up top. Soon a path was opening up. Caleigh climbed down first, then Jenny. Andrew opted to stay and help David with overhead cover fire.

"Master Chief, *go* I will give you cover fire!" David said. "Get to the others!"

Master Chief lowered all his guns and ammo on a separate line and then slid down to the ground like a hiker on a cliff. Jenny and Caleigh, armed with pistols, ran to Jenny's helicopter so Jenny could get a smoke flair as a signal. Caleigh did her best to shoot so many on the flight deck. Jenny ran as fast as she could as David shot her a path, hitting the ones in front of her. As she approached the helicopter, the infected fell to the hands of David. Caleigh grabbed another clip from her back pocket. As she clicked it in, she forgot to slide the first round in the chamber. Her mistake made the zombie jump on her and bite her on the back. David reloaded and shot the zombie eating her. Seeing her fall to the hands made David think that his effort was pointless. He was enraged with anger as about thirty of them swarmed on Caleigh, eating her while she was still alive. These savages ripped Caleigh's arms off and aggressively gorged on her flesh.

Boats ran around, opening the side and making a hole. With his guns blazing, he headed around the corner and ran into Master Chief.

"Woah!" Master Chief said. "What a relief to see you here."

"Same here," Boats replied. "Where is the rescue?"

Jenny opened the slide door and grabbed out the emergency rescue kit, rummaging through it. She grabbed three smoke flares, cracked one, and threw it. The red smoke rose in the air as the bright flare could be seen. Zombies, attracted to the noise, went after the flair. Looking up in the sky, she saw the Raptors less than a minute away. The Raptors flew overhead, roaring.

Master Chief grinned, "Every time they appear, destruction soon follows!"

Sure enough they launched missiles at the grounded planes on the flight deck. This created a huge inferno, causing a chain reaction of explosions. Planes once used for the air were now being destroyed. The infected were also being taken out as well as hundreds of them were engulfed in flames. The zombies going after Boats ran from the explosions.

Jenny ran as fast as she could to get away from the fires. A loud explosion, not even fifteen feet from her, went off. A shrapnel went into her leg. Everyone heard her scream bloody murder as the pain was unbearable. Boats, and Master Chief ran to her aid. David was still up top, picking off infected and burning ones. He heard a loud crash as some of the crawlers made their way on the bridge. He turned around and saw Andrew Barich desperately trying to fight them off. Andrew threw one on the floor. Another, not wasting any time, jumped on his back, biting his neck, and two more jumped up. Andrew was brought to one knee. David saw them eating him alive, biting his face, his skin. Andrew stood up with about five of them on top of him. He ran as best as he could, knowing that once he was bitten he would turn. The zombies held on to him, determined to take him down. Near the edge, Andrew jumped to his death, taking all five of them with him. Even as he fell, he fought them, getting his last-minute strikes in until he smashed on the flight deck. The impact killed him instantly and the infected fell to their doom as well.

Soon the bridge was full of zombies all active and running toward David. He had to think quickly. He jumped down the line Master Chief used. He slid dow, but a jumper lunged on him while he was halfway down and bit his hands, making David fall off about twenty-five feet into the horde waiting on the bottom. David was quickly devoured.

The confusion separated Ward and the remaining survivors from Boats, Timmy, Master Chief, Billy, and Jenny.

Debris of burning wrecks created a wall for the survivors. There were loud rumbles as thousands were on their way. This loud explosion attracted possibly all of the infected.

Jenny gave Boats the second flare. He took it and threw it, creating another smoke signal.

The horde went after Ward and the remaining survivors. Boats and Timmy lay in wait as they heard them eating everyone. There was nothing they could do. Once they finished with Ward and his group, the infected would come for the last remaining living.

Billy was put next to Jenny. Since she could not do much, she was in charge of reloading the guns when the horde arrived. Boats and Timmy grabbed all the ammo and guns they could carry.

"Well, guys, they are five minutes late," said Master Chief. "I don't think they are coming." As he stood up with the M240 gun, he opened fire. His bullets hit the zombies as they charged, ripping them to shreds. The jumpers charged, leaping over the massive discharge of bullets. In the air, they were vulnerable as Boats and Timmy picked them easily from the sky.

The sun was about to set, and the horde waited. They did not advance. Something kept them at bay. About a hundred feet beyond the burning fires, they could be heard screaming as if they were rallying another charge. Only the fire kept them separated. The semicircle of debris of about fiftty feet was where the remaining five were. Reloading their guns, they knew that this would be it. This was where they would keep them back, all the way until the end. Billy awoke as all the excitement was about to unfold.

"Guys, why did you save me?" he asked.

"The United States wants you alive, buddy," Master Chief responded.

"Kill me, please," Billy begged.

"What?" Boats said. "No, we won't kill—"

"They will use me as a weapon," Billy interrupted. "This will never end. Please kill me. I am the reason for all of this."

Jenny crawled to him, holding his hand. Master Chief looked at Boats and Timmy as if they all agreed. Jenny faced the other way, crying as Timmy pulled out his gun and shot Billy in the head. If anyone was going to kill Billy, it would be Timmy. Maybe this was the revenge for his family he was denied.

"Okay, so how are we going to explain this one?" Master Chief asked.

"It's not like we're getting saved," Boats said. "Looks like the horde is getting ready for another wave. We better arm up."

The mood was quiet as Master Chief grabbed the 12-gauge shotgun and pulled out his cigar. This was supposed to be smoked once they were rescued. He may not have a chance to ever smoke a Cuban ever again.

Boats and Timmy reloaded the pistols and M16 guns. Jenny was instructed to continue to reload all weapons all the way until the end.

Boats was armed with four pistols and two M16 guns. He stuck the pistols in his back belt and two on the side. It would have to do as he had no holsters. Laying one of the M16 next to his feet, he fully reloaded one.

Timmy had the same idea. His pistols were side by side in front of his feet, ready to be grabbed once the ammo ran out. Full clips were placed, about fifteen of them, for easy reload. Jenny continued to reload empty clips, getting them ready. Master Chief moved to the left, about twenty-five feet away to provide extra firepower in case they breached the wall of debris.

Lightning could be seen at a distance from the east as thunder rolled from the dark clouds while a beautiful sunset was occurring to the west. A storm was approaching as they prepared for battle.

The loud roar echoed as the horde sent in the first wave of hundreds. The rumble of the stampede shook the deck as they charged. Timmy stood ready ten feet to the Boats's left. Looking at Timmy, Boats spoke, "Hey, Timmy, I want you to know I would rather find no other death more satisfying than next to you in battle."

"Don't get all soft on me Boats!" Timmy replied.

It was then that Boats realized Timmy was just like him, salty, full of sharp edges. He was just as proud at how mature he grew within the past two days of excitement. "Hey, I am sorry about Cindy," he said.

The horde could be heard getting closer.

"After I punched you, I reasoned with my conscience. There was nothing I could do. I know this now. It was not your fault. I forgave myself." Timmy wiped his eyes.

"Timmy, don't get all soft on me!" Boats retorted.

They slightly grinned at each other as the horde approached, now only fifty feet and closing, their teeth full of black decay as blood spewed from their mouths. Their sloppy run made them bump into each other. The weak got knocked over and were immediately trampled.

"HERE THEY COME!" Boats shouted. "IT'S ONLY A FEW HUNDRED! THEY LOOK LIKE THEY ARE COMING IN WAVES! EVERYONE GET READY!"

# Chapter 14

## *THE FINAL STAND*

The guns rippled into the horde as the bullets stopped them. There were bloody explosions as brains and guns splattered from the hands of Boats and Timmy. Twenty of them jumped the debris only to have Master Chief pump them with the shotgun. The close range severed limbs. It sounded like a war zone as guns were fired into the infected. The automatic M16 ripped heads one by one, yet wave after wave they still charged. Timmy double-checked for any movement in case any got missed. He quickly ended those crawlers as well. Two more jumped for Master Chief as they misjudged this salty bastard. He punched one on the face with the back of his shotgun, pumped another round, and fired from behind, hitting another in the face.

Boats timed his shots. Holding the M16 in one hand and putting it on his hip, he fired. The other hand had a pistol in it, finishing up the horde. Timmy aimed well, making sure each infected he struck fell to the ground. The bodies lay on the deck as more charged. Any empty clips were thrown to Jenny who quickly reloaded them. A roar soon could be heard from an unknown zombie as the rest listened and fell back. Boats saw them retreating as he aimed his M16 at the fueling tank of one of the crippled plane. The explosion sent Boats flying on his back, and Timmy covered his face from the heat. The fire burned, keeping the rest of the horde at bay.

"It's only a matter of time when they charge again," Timmy said.

"I think they know a front attack is pointless," said Boats.

"What happens when they all charge at once?" Master Chief asked as he reloaded his shells into the shotgun.

"We're getting low on ammo, huh, Jenny?" Boats asked.

"Yeah, we're getting low," she confirmed.

"I think if they charge again," Boats began, "we won't be able to hold them. We will get breached."

"Well then, we go out fighting. I don't think the rescue is coming," said Master Chief.

There was another loud roar as the horde soon pressed onward once again. The fires engulfed them, and they were now easy pickings. About fifty of them ran through the fires only to burn to death and have bullets pierce their charred skulls.

"Looks like they are going to wait," Timmy observed. "Too many of them are burning themselves to death."

"As long as the fire burns, they won't charge. This will buy us some time," Master Chief said.

Timmy looked at Boats with desperation as Boats he was going to get them out of this. Maybe some secret exit or extra clips would appear in their last stand on earth. Only four remained. Only four survivors were left.

Just in front of the fire, three of them stopped about twenty feet from the undead whose eyes were missing, teeth broken from unsuccessfully biting through metal or worn from chewing on bones. The decaying of their skin was as if they were walking the earth for over hundreds of years. Their hands were not that of a human but more like rotting limbs ready to fall off. They could not see at all. Their eyes were black and white, with fungus growing where human eyeballs once gazed and were now replaced with a horrible curse. Their heads turned in every direction, but their smell was not that good either. However, their hearing was acute. Just the sound of the fire crackling was enough to alert their senses.

The crack of the gun echoed, loud enough to get their attention to where only two now stood, and behind them were hundreds, if not thousands, of the cursed. The remaining two crouched on all fours, smelling the one that was shot, and they and ran toward the loud noise. Timmy stood there waiting to time his shots—he remembered what Boats told him about wasting shots. One of them jumped arms extended, leaping fifteen feet in the air like a lion pouncing on its prey, toward Timmy. As the cursed descended on the human, another loud gunshot echoed. The cursed one got pushed back by the force of a 12-gauge shotgun pumping pellets through his skull. Master Chief grinned as he pumped another shell into the chamber. There was nothing left of the undead's face, only a headless mess of splattered blood and brain pieces. *One more to kill, then we will battle our final stand,* Boats thought to himself. *These must have been the scouts before another wave. No rest now. Once this last one lies before their feet, the fury of the devil himself will bestow only misery on the remaining.* Boats aimed carefully as the last one charged like a lion, grunting with infected saliva spewing from its mouth. Every move he made excreted piles of blood dripping from his mouth. Boats aimed down his sights and fired, jerking his arm back, and the cursed was shot down as the bullet pierced the skull into the spine. "Reload! Reload, everyone! Here they come!" Boats cried.

Echoes of the dead drowned the mere scream coming from Boats. They ran as fast as they could as if it was their last meal. The undead charged, trampling over each other, often fighting and pushing and biting each other, just to get a taste of human flesh. The horde was charging.

Master Chief reloaded the shotgun once again. With a cigar in the left side of his mouth, this salty fucker would not go down easily. His old-school ways were uncanny. Even now as they charged at him, he glanced toward the west to watch the sunset and remembered how things got so fucked up. The talent this old man had clearly showed—superb marksmanship. He never flinched a timed shot as he just decapitated three of them with his 12-gauge pump-action shotgun. Still for a second, his eyes did not gaze away from the sun as it crept below the ocean horizon. From the east, a storm was building. All that remained was the invasion of the darkness from the east. "Lieutenant, I need you here with me. Don't go UA on me yet!" Even in the face of death, this crusty master chief still honored military bearing.

She nodded her head and checked her rounds to make sure she had enough for the end. A previous explosion sent a large piece of shrapnel through her leg, her left thigh. It was evident that if it was pulled out, it would cut off a major blood artery, possibly killing her within minutes. Her job now was to load up the guns and pass them to what was left of the survivors. Her leg throbbed in pain, but she guessed that it was better than being a walking lifeless being.

Timmy yelled at boats, "Boats, remember when I asked you to kill me if I ever turned?" Boats acted like he didn't hear as he neared only two shots left. Timmy yelled again, "Boats, I know you fucking hear me! You remember what you promised me if I ever turned?" Boats nodded and already knew what Timmy was going to ask him to do. His last shot he pointed toward the cursed and hesitated. Boats knew that if he did not do this, he was going to end up killing his buddy after he turned. His face accepted what fate lay before them. Turning his last shot towards Timmy, he thought how strange it was to look down the sights and not see and infected. Boats shouted, "Timmy, do it to me as well!"

Without hesitance, Timmy drew his last shot and aimed it at Boats. It had to have been mere seconds apart. The last round was forced into the chamber, ready to serve its final purpose. The cocking of the final metal click that the chamber round made assured them both that all this would be over in a matter of seconds.

Without hesitating, Timmy drew his last shot and aimed it at Boats.

"We had a great ride!" Boats yelled. Looking directly at Timmy he could hear hundreds coming within feet of tearing both of them to shreds. Master Chief could see what was about to unfold. There was no way he could stop this suicide. His screams could not be heard, nor could he prevent how Timmy and Boats were going to end their lives. An unfamiliar humming drew close. Was this another evolution of them? The sound got louder and louder, almost shaking the ground. Fear was going to take over. Before that was allowed, actions had to be executed. Rather than turn to the direction of the loud noise, Timmy smiled and said, "It's too bad. Tonight was pizza night." Both slightly laughed, and with his last sigh of breath, he counted out loud.

Boats mimicked his lips saying *three*, and they aimed at each other. *Two*, the final round was clicked into the chamber and the safety remained off. *One . . .*

The gun from Timmy's hand was damaged as a bullet hit it, knocking it out of his hand. The instant it hit, Timmy moved two paces to the right and heard Boats's bullet whiz right past where he was standing within a half a second. Looking up in the air, a giant shadow loomed down on them. Red lasers pointed at them. The spotlight was now on the remaining survivors. Looking up, they threw their hands up as a sign of surrender. The loud humming noise came from the whipping propellers of the rescue chopper hovering above them. The horde jumped at them, but reinforcement firepower descended from the unfamiliar military chopper. Two 25MM Gatling guns cleared the path, destroying anything it aimed at. A single 40MM Bofors gun, capable of wiping out a twenty-five-foot radius, was fired at the horde. The rescue was underway. A line dropped down as a lone guy dressed in all black padding was lowered on to the flight deck. He crouched low. Keeping his weapon close to his eye, he dropped at least fifteen zombies within mere seconds. He then waved his finger in a circular motion, and four more lines dropped with reinforcements.

More of these men followed. They dropped on the flight deck, creating a semicircle around the survivors. Jenny and Master Chief breathed as they saw the massive firepower these six soldiers unleashed. The choppers were providing additional support from the air. One of them, whose face was covered in black and wearing black goggles, spoke to Timmy, "Excuse me. We are U.S. Navy Seal Team Four. We are looking for Master Chief. Is he alive?" Timmy pointed at where Jenny was. The Navy Seal nodded and went over to Jenny. Next to her was Master Chief, dealing with hand-to-weapon combat, engaging the infected. The SEAL pulled out his automatic pistol, killing the zombies around Master Chief. "Excuse me, Master Chief, do you have the guy and the file?" the voice said.

Master Chief reached in his pocket and gave him the memory stick that Timmy gave to him. As the Navy SEAL went to grab it, Master Chief pulled it back, screaming over the chopper's roaring blades," DO I HAVE YOUR WORD THAT YOU'D GET THESE GUYS OUT OF HERE?"

The SEAL nodded his head. He then heard someone talking in his earpiece and grabbed Master Chief, "Where is Billy?" Master Chief pointed to where his dead body lay. "No matter. We take him dead or alive." He wrapped a line around Billy's corpse, and they hauled him into the chopper and tied him down. The SEAL then grabbed Master Chief and wrapped a line around him and said, "You need to come with us. Don't worry. The other choppers will grab them." The signal hand was given, and Master Chief was abruptly hauled into the chopper. From his view, he could see the devastation on the flight deck.

Jenny looked up as the wind from the blades was blowing debris everywhere. She waved to Master Chief as if to thank him.

Sitting in the attack chopper, Master Chief hung his legs outside as the helicopter ascended up into the clouds. "Oh my god!" he said as he saw thousands of them scampering from all directions around the flight deck. The SEALs were doing their part keeping them back. Once the helicopter was about two thousand feet up, another helicopter approached the survivors and was descending near their location. The chopper Master Chief was in cut hard right and accelerated. That was the last view Master Chief saw of the crippled carrier. Laying his head on the back of the chopper's wall, he closed his eyes. All he wanted to do was rest.

A gentleman from the front cockpit crawled back and sat across Master Chief. He screamed over the rotating blades as he introduced himself as Mr. Rene Barrier, a political advisor to the head senators from Washington. He was an older man in his midfifties. His black suit and red tie made him look out of place in the combat area. He spoke, extending his hand, "Master Chief? It is an honor to meet you."

"Good to meet you, sir," Master Chief said.

"I come from the Pentagon. What a mess we have here. Do you not agree?"

"Yes, sir."

"We owe you a great gratitude for what you have done for our country. Do you have the files?"

"Yes, sir." Master Chief reached in his pocket since he was satisfied the others made it. "Here you go, sir. Everything is on it."

"What happened to Billy?"

"He didn't make it."

"No matter. What a fucking mess we have to fix!"

"What do you mean?"

"That is of no concern to you. Now tell me"—he put his arm around Master Chief—"what do you know about . . . what happened.

"I know everything."

"I understand. I want you to know we owe you a great gratitude of what you have done for our country. Thank you for your services to your country."

Turning close to him, he fired a gun he had hidden in his jacket. Master Chief was shot in the chest. He felt the sudden blast sever his lungs as he tried to grasp what happened. Looking at his chest, he now saw blood all over his shirt. Another shot went off three more times. He could not believe what just happened. Everything he done in his life was summed up as he smelt the smoke from the gun rise from his chest. Thirty-three years, and this is how his country repaid a hero? As he fell back, he held on to the strap. Mr. Barrier took a cloth and cleaned off the gun and threw it to one of the SEALs in the chopper.

The SEAL, disgusted with the events that just happened, threw the gun out the window. Mr. Barrier looked at Master Chief holding on to the strap, the only thing that kept him from falling out the chopper.

"I am truly sorry," Barrier said, "but this is beyond your doing, and certain political funds and upcoming elections will not be stalled. May God bless you for what you did for our country. You are a true American Hero"

With that, Master Chief fell back. Letting go of the strap, he fell into the ocean abyss. One of the SEALs tried to grab him but ripped off his dog tags instead. Looking at the tags that were now covered in blood, he gripped them as he watched Master Chief fall out of the chopper to his ocean grave.

Barrier then said to them, "You guys do what your told. This was coming from your bosses too. That guy Billy? Dump the body in the ocean. There cannot be any trace of this."

With one heave, the body was released. As the helicopter flew by into the distance of the horizon, the waves swallowed up the bodies of the dead.

# Chapter 15

## *The Beginning of the End*

Boats and Timmy ran to Jenny, staying close to her as the remaining SEALs pushed back the horde. As Jenny saw Master Chief's helicopter leave the war zone, another chopper approached, providing more covering fire. One of the SEALs jabbed a needle in Jenny's thigh, giving her a jolt of morphine.

"Ouch! What the fuck!" Jenny said.

"I gave you a happy drug," the SEAL said. "No piss tests, okay?" And he gave her the okay finger.

The SEAL motioned that it was time to go. The SEALs then fell back to the chopper. Timmy and Boats grabbed Jenny and followed. One of the SEALs stopped them and told them the reality. "Guys, get away from the chopper. This was never a rescue operation."

"What do you mean?" Boats asked. "We are not infected!"

"I am sorry," the SEAL said. "We have our orders. This was *never* a rescue. We were here to rescue only one person, and that person is safely aboard the other chopper."

"NO!" Timmy shouted. "This is fucking bullshit! Don't fucking let us die here!"

The SEALs pointed their guns at Boats and Timmy and offered them another alternative. A quick pull of the trigger and it would all be over. Falling back to the chopper, they boarded and ascended into the clouds. The wind picked up debris, blowing dirt everywhere. Boats and Timmy fell back to Jenny who was feeling pretty good from the double dose of morphine.

"Fuck, the helicopter is still good," Jenny said. "We can get away."

"Shit, how much time you need?" Boats asked.

"Here, Boats, take this flare. They will run to the light. Break it about a hundred yards away from the chopper. That will give me time to get airborne."

"Ma'am if you pull this off . . ." Boats trailed off. "Fine, I will give you time."

As Boats ran, the infected went for him as he jumped over the debris. Dodging their clawlike hands, he ran like a receiver running for a touchdown in the end zone, except this time his life depended on it.

The infected ran toward Boats's front, completely surrounding him. As they closed on him, he could see the visions of hungry flesh-eating creatures inches from his face. The final defeat was inevitable. Boats would not get out of this one. Closing his eyes, he clenched his fists, readying himself for the first strike. As he grinned and waited for the first blow, the SEAL Team chopper opened fire, taking out the zombies near him. The shots from the automatic Gatling gun were flawless. Not one shot hit Boats as the dead were decapitated all around him. Looking up at the SEALS, he waved to them. They were giving him some kind of chance. If they could not rescue them, they would offer assistance. Breaking the smoke flares Boats threw it as the zombies focused towards the bright light. The loud whistle of the roaring flair attracted flanks of the undead towards its direction.

Timmy helped Jenny to her feet, putting his arm around her so she could lean on him and get to the chopper. After helping her inside the cockpit, he ran around. An infected ran for Jenny, grabbing her leg. She panicked and reached quickly, slamming the door over and over, crushing his deformed face. Blood sprayed everywhere as he let go of her and fell to his death. Timmy jumped in the other side, asking her what was wrong. She was covered in zombie blood from the infected.

"Holy shit!" Timmy exclaimed. "Are you bitten?"

"No, I am fine. He didn't get me. It's his blood. He tried to grab my leg, but I—never mind, get the chain holder off. I don't care if you have to shoot them."

Timmy jumped out and grabbed a shotgun that Master Chief left and shot the chains that were holding the chopper in place. Once they were all clear, he jumped back in and put on the headphones. Jenny, already starting up the engines, watched the oil pressure as it heated up. The whip of the propellers created massive wind, creating a loud engine noise as the helicopter rose slowly off the ground.

Using the stick, she leveled out the tail for optimum lift. As the plane ascended, they could see the entire devastation from the air. Swinging the helicopter around, Jenny came around for a pass. The view from the helicopter showed thousands of the infected chasing Boats near the bow of the carrier.

"Hold on, Timmy," Jenny said. "I'm going to mow the grass."

"NO!" Timmy exclaimed. "You're not going to do what I think you are—OH SHIT!"

As the helicopter evened out behind the, horde Jenny tipped the front straight down, and the propeller blades grinded only feet away from the deck. Pushing forward, she directed the blades right into the horde chasing Boats, cutting them up like fruit in a blender. The horde didn't stand a chance as hundreds of body parts went scattering everywhere.

Boats heard the propellers, and he jumped on his stomach. The blades went right over him as the helicopter flew overhead.

"HELL FUCKING YEAH! COME GET SOME!" Timmy shouted.

Jenny then said, "Timmy, get a line ready. There is still a lot chasing Boats. Get your ass in the back and get ready to grab him."

Timmy nodded as he noticed blood gushing out of Jenny's injured leg. He ignored it and jumped in the back. Wrapping a line around his waist, he made sure that if she turned hard, he would be secure even if both side doors were open. He was tied to the helicopter. Worse case was he falls out, and the line saves him.

Grabbing an extra line, he tied a bowline with a loop about four feet in diameter and hung it out the right side of the window. The helicopter was above Boats. Boats ran as he saw the line fall out. The horde was still in hot pursuit, trying to kill him. Boats sprinted as fast as he could. Getting to the bow of the ship, he leaped for the line and grabbed the loop. The loop, once tensioned tightened up around his wrist, assuring they had him. Jenny pulled the helicopter vertically straight. Boats held on for the ride.

The horde below him screamed in agony, wanting to just eat flesh one more time before he left the ship. Timmy pulled up the line one stroke at a time and then grabbed Boat's hand, pulling him in the back. The helicopter circled the carrier. From the air, the entire flight deck could be seen, all the destruction, all the fires and countless dead bodies that fell to the hands of Boats and Timmy.

Timmy sat on his butt and jumped. "Ouch! What the hell?" Checking in his back pants pocket, he discovered a memory stick. Lambert must have stuck it in there.

"I wonder if he gave Master Chief a fake, or there if he made two copies," Boats said.

"Once we get to a computer, we will find out," replied Timmy. "I need to check on Jenny."

As he crouched, walking to the front where Jenny was, he smacked Boats in the back of the head as if to say, "We made it. We are alive."

Boats sat back and decided to rest his eyes. As the moon reflected on the ocean, a school of dolphins could be seen below, disturbing the calm waters as they came up for air. Boats was at peace with himself. After all that has happened, it was finally over.

Jenny flew silently, with tears running down her face. She grabbed her iPod that was left in the helicopter before the infection. Finding Bon

Jovi, she played "Wanted Dead or Alive" on the loud speakers as she steered her course to find the nearest land.

Timmy stayed in the co-pilot seat and was worried because Jenny kept dozing off. Her head kept bobbing as she tried to stay awake. The shrapnel severely injured her leg. "Ma'am, are you going to be okay?" Timmy asked.

"Yes," Jenny replied. "I . . . I am fine. Get some rest. I will be okay.

"I'm Seaman Timmy," he said, introducing himself for the first time.

"I am Lieutenant Jenifer McCormick," she replied. "nice to meet you."

"Thank you for—"

"It's okay. We all lost a lot. Do you have family?"

"I did, but I lost her on the ship."

"I don't understand . . ."

"I was dating someone on the ship. Her name was Cindy Walkers."

There was an awkward silence as Jenny was trying to be friendly to her co-pilot. "I am sorry," she finally said.

"She was pregnant, and I found out too late."

"I am so sorry. I had no idea."

"It's okay. I have made my peace. How about you? Are you married? Kids?"

Jenny chuckled. "No, I . . . well no, my career kind of got in the way. I don't think I made my parents happy."

"Look, don't feel bad. Think of all the people that have no idea what happened back on the ship? All the wives and husbands kids that will never see their loved ones again. We are the fortunate ones."

"I never looked at it like that," she said. "Hey, you get some rest. According to my instruments, we need to find fuel before—never mind, we need to just make it safe."

Timmy did his best to keep awake as exhaustion finally set in. His eyes grew heavy as there was no sign of land yet. His thoughts went back to Cindy and how much he missed her. It was there that he mourned her loss. He lost his family. Tears rolled down as he closed his eyes.

He nursed the vision of the last night he spent with Cindy as he lay with her under the sheets. It was the dream of the day before they left on deployment. She lay next to Timmy with her hair over her face. She smiled and told him how she wanted to be with him. As she kissed him, he felt her soft lips on his. Her eyes closed as it was peaceful. She called his name, "Timothy, Timothy, wake up!" as he looked, she was ripped out of his arms, out of the bed, and out of his thoughts. He awoke to the helicopter spinning out of control.

The loud beep awoke Timmy. Jenny was slouched over, not moving. The tail of the plane was spinning uncontrollably. Timmy felt for a pulse. She picked up her head and turned her neck to the right, looking at him.

"Lieutenant?" Timmy asked. "Are you okay, ma'am? Answer me? Are you okay?"

Growling, she revealed her bloody teeth and lunged for him. Timmy jumped back. He looked at her leg and noticed bite marks. She had been infected earlier. Her face, once pretty, was now spitting blood and trying to bite him.

"Oh shit!" he shouted. "BOATS HELP ME!"

Timmy tried to grab the stick between her legs to control the helicopter, but she was to aggressive, trying to bite his arms on every little attempt he tried.

Boats was unconscious from a head impact when he hit the side of the door. Opening the door, Timmy looked back at Boats flying around like a rag doll. He reached in the back and cut Boat's safety line. The velocity of the spinning flung Boats out the side door. That was the last time Timmy would see Boats.

His decision of cutting Boats was from thinking that either he'd die inside the crashing helicopter or the he'd have a slight chance that he'd survive his fall.

Jenny, now in a rage, was kicking, working her way out the safety belt. Timmy screamed. As he slid in the back, he could see the front window facing straight into the ground. He decided to stay in the helicopter in order to avoid being cut by the propeller blades. The helicopter crashed, and smoke rose, a hundred-foot mushroom of debris. Timmy was thrown from the wreck, landing hard on his back. The impact knocked the wind out of him. The gas tank ignited, sending what was salvageable of the helicopter up in smoke.

Timmy lay there on the ground for a good minute. Gathering his bearings, he felt a sharp pain near his ribs. As he opened up his shirt, he discovered that metal shrapnel penetrated through his skin. A sharp metal piece was stuck in as he lay there in pain. It was horrible. He knew the piece must be removed immediately or it will cause severe infection. Grabbing the jagged metal object wedged in his rib, he screamed in pain. Even just a slight touch was sending the metal deeper. Tears fell as the pain was too much to bear.

"FUCK! FUCK!" he cursed. "THIS HAS TO COME OUT, OH JESUS GOD!"

Ripping his shirt, he stuffed a piece in his mouth to bite down on. The simple breathing was killing him. As his breath increased, his heart raced, but he went on and prepared for the removal of the shrapnel. Biting on the rag, he grabbed the piece. "Okay," he breathed. "okay.One, two, three! He held his breath and ripped the metal piece out, screaming in pain.

Shock was setting in. Looking up at the sunrise, he felt at peace. He lay there. As he was about to pass out, he could see something hover over him, the blood spatters hitting his forehead. This was not a rescue. It was infected Jenny. He did not scream but accepted the inevitable. The end was now. As she loomed over him, blocking the sun with her silhouette, Timmy blacked out.

. . . . .

Boats felt the hot sun beating on his face as crows flew overhead. He heard them cawing at him. His eyes focused as he lay there, on his stomach. He rolled over and felt the sharp pain and discomfort in his right shoulder. It popped out of the join from the crash. The pain was unbearable.

He didn't remember how he landed here. All he remembered was waking up to the tail spinning out of control, and a $CO_2$ bottle unhooked and hit him on the side of the head, instantly knocking him out. His last vision was seeing Timmy cut him free, and he fell out the helicopter. Most people survive long falls if their bodies stay limp and relaxed as did Boats when he plummeted to earth.

Now he awoke to the vast nothing of his new surroundings. There was no one around him, just red sand for as far as the eye could see. He sat up and his right arm hung limp. He used his left arm to balance himself on his feet. Standing up, he adjusted his eyes to the environment. He walked alone. There was no one around him, nothing to see. He hollered, "HELLO! ANYONE, HELLO!" But he only heard his own voice's echo as it faded in the distance. Boats had no idea where he was or how he got so far from the wreck.. The hit on the head was worse than he thought.

He slowly walked about two miles up the dirt road. His muscles ached with pain and uncomfortable sores. He walked toward the sign he could see in the distance. His lips dried from the sweltering sun, and he was in agony each step he made he was now feeling the pain of the crash on his body. He kept looking for the wreck but there was nothing as far as the eye could see.

Looking at his watch, he saw it was 10:00 am. He had no idea where he was. All he knew was if he could only read the sign, he could figure out where the nearest town was. Forty-five minutes later he stumbled to the sign next to the dirt road as the buzzards flew overhead, waiting for Boats to fall.

He thought of where the hell we was and how he ended up alone. It was all interrupted by the row of abandoned cars on the side of the dirt road. He could hear the radio playing Johnny Cash;Ring of Fire in one of the abandoned cars. He walked up to one of them that was already burned to a crisp. There was nothing left of whoever owned it. And all that happened replayed in his mind as he saw the sign much closer and more focused In shock, Boats fell to his knees in denial. This can't be happening. Nothing made sense as he tried to recall. His mind was a blank, the torn uniform serving no purpose, and the dislocated right arm hung with agonizing pain as it served no purpose.

The sign read, Australia . . . . Sydney 15 km," but it was the writing that was painted over the sign that puzzled him. It was smeared in blood, and it simply read,

# Entering the City
## of the Dead

To Be Continued....

Printed in the USA
CPSIA information can be obtained
at www.ICGtesting.com
LVHW040023231023
761837LV00018BA/124/J